A Horse Came Running

A Horse
Came Running

BY MEINDERT DeJONG

COLLIER BOOKS
New York, New York

The Macmillan Company
866 Third Avenue, New York, New York 10022

Collier-Macmillan Canada Ltd., Toronto, Ontario

Library of Congress catalog card number: 71–99119

This book is also published in an illustrated
hardcover edition by The Macmillan Company.

First Collier Books Edition 1972
Second Printing 1972

Printed in the United States of America

To Tom and Amy Hubbard
Who also served—
They waited long enough.

"It is enough
to be so;
the wind
blows between."

From "O Child, Child,"
by Frederick ten Hoor

Contents

A Horse Came Running

1

To Race a Train

Two horses were standing at their pasture fence. The old horse was waiting, the young horse, new to the place, was merely staying close. The old horse seemed to be looking toward the big white house that rose at the end of the pasture, but he was really looking beyond toward a hill around which the evening train must come. He stood stamping, tail switching, impatient to begin his twice-daily game of racing the twice-daily train the length of the pasture.

The new horse came closer as if to rest her neck across his but then, as if that was too much familiarity, she turned away and rested her neck on one of the fence posts instead. She stared across the railroad tracks at a grove of big trees but saw nothing. She was only waiting to take her cue from the old horse. Then, like this morning and yesterday—her first day —she would run easily alongside the pounding old horse and the pounding, loaded train.

She knew that they would bring themselves up just short of crashing into the fence at the end of the pasture. Then the train would roll on relentlessly and they would return to their grazing, side by side—that was all the new horse needed or wanted in her homesick heaviness.

The late afternoon seemed to stand as sad and as sluggish as the new horse. There was an odd pressure and a sullenness. Deep within that sullenness lay a silent threat.

A flock of twittering small birds came sweeping over the pasture, swooped low over the horses and buried themselves in the grove of big trees across the railroad tracks. For long moments the full-leafed trees stirred with the burrowing birds. Then the birds, too, were still, as if gone to roost, as if night were coming in the late afternoon.

At that quiet moment, train sounds came to the ears of the old horse. But the sounds were too far and too thin to begin his first move. His black broom tail hung stiff and quiet. This was the quivery moment before the train would come around the hill—the breathless pause —before the sudden wheeling and the powerful charge along the pasture fence. The other horse, too new and strange to be keenly aware of train sounds, stayed staring at the trees of the little birds.

Then came a roar—the roar as of a hundred rushing trains. But no train came. Instead, over the top of the distant hill rose a black, whipping, funnel-shaped cloud. On it came, swinging, slinging its great evil snout— reaching out to devour everything in the helpless countryside. In white-eyed terror the horses raced ahead of it.

Far behind the horses the door of the big white house was thrown open and a man came running down the steps. He called back to the house, "Lin, come help me get that new horse of yours, she's scared and if the tornado *does* come this way we'll . . ." A young girl rushed out on the porch, "Daddy!" she called, "the radio says it's headed this way! We won't have time to . . ." She whirled at the roar behind her. "It's here, it's here!" she screamed, and pointed, then dashed back into the house.

The man turned and saw the black funnel dipping toward the house. He cleared the steps

3

in one jump, ran in the house, grabbed the girl by one hand and came out with her. "It's safer in the stable," he yelled as they ran. "Lie flat on the floor," he gasped as he pushed her inside and slammed the door of the stable.

The whirling funnel came down, enveloped the big white house, sucked it up and rose with it, high in the air. The splintering house within the black maw added its own scream to the shriek and the horror.

The tornado had taken the house off its basement walls but the stable stood untouched back of the house under a clump of trees.

Now, as the tornado lifted, it was as if it saw the plunging horses at the pasture's end. Down it dipped again, flinging a roof beam, a twisted stove, beds, tables and a white refrigerator from its snout. The dropped things smashed or speared into the ground, helter-skelter the length of the pasture.

On it came, and the horses could only plunge madly back and forth as they tried to escape. The old horse whinnied and tried to break through the fence, but the heavy wire threw him back and he fell to the ground. The new horse turned and ran in frantic fear as the tornado sucked the old horse up into itself. Behind her, sections of fence pulled into the air.

She tore ahead of the disappearing fence, snorting her terror. Suddenly her feet were not on the ground. She, too, was in the air, hoofs pawing, legs pistoning, caught in the outer edge of the funnel. Then the tornado shifted, dropped her back to the ground and turned out of the pasture toward the grove of trees across the tracks.

The new horse landed on all four legs, stuttered a few wooden steps, then stood in dazed shock as the tornado whipped the lash of its tail among the trees of the little birds.

Before her eyes the great trees began to scream and twist up out of the ground. They whined up, tossed for a moment, then smashed down on their branches in a tangled heap. Just beyond them the tornado dropped the old horse. He, too, lay upside down and horribly still.

Then, as if she had just found she could move, the new horse backed away from the spooking horror of the dead horse and the giant roots clawing whitely up into the sky. Further on, the tornado dipped into a gully and thrashed there unseen like a roaring, idiot giant. After long moments it rose high into the air and moved away.

With a snort the backing horse came out of

her shock, whirled and charged toward the stable. Somehow she avoided the debris the tornado had scattered in the pasture, but the basement walls of the gone, white house brought her up short and quivering. She stared at the naked, strange walls, and instead of turning toward the safety of the stable, she wheeled away.

In her sudden turning she leaped a white refrigerator that lay smashed in her path. She cleared it but she cut her ankle on a chisel-sharp piece of metal pointing up from the out-flung door. In new, hurt madness she plowed through a bush in the front yard. A woman's dress was caught in its branches. The filmy stuff wrapped itself around her leg, pasted and stuck there in the thick, guttering blood from the cut. The hem of the dress fluttering under her made her plunge and sunfish wildly.

Unable to get away from the fluttering cloth she broke into a blind run. Accidentally she took the path the tornado had come—a mowed, swept path of destruction. Finally she crossed an asphalt road and was about to run down it, when a farmyard water trough slid out of the top of a tree and clanged down in front of her.

Eyes rolling, nostrils gaping, she fled once more up the path of the tornado. On and on she ran, not aware of exhaustion until she came to a steep hill. But then, suddenly, as if only now aware of her hurt leg, she stopped a moment and then limped slowly up the hill. There she stopped again and looked around. Far across the fields she saw an unwrecked barn whose great hay doors stood open. She started toward them.

As she crossed into the field she came to a gully at the end of a small wood. There in the gully lay more twisted trees—and there, too, was a horse. An old, white horse. But this horse was not dead. This horse was on his feet, imprisoned in the tangle of trees.

Slow step by slow step she backed away from the white horse and the white roots pointing in the air. At last she was able to turn away, but, instead of going to the barn with its wide-open doors, she angled off at an uneasy jog around the gully and ended up in the small woodlot.

The little wood was still, everything was upright and untouched. She went in among the quiet trees. The old horse in the gully whinnied after her pathetically, but she did not answer him—she did not seem to hear. She jogged away into the darkness under the safe, strong trees.

She came to a small creek and walked into it, unseeing. The sudden coldness of the water shocked her to a stop. She stood trembling. The horse in the gully whinnied once more, but she did not answer. She stood in safe darkness—the creek gurgled soft, babyish sounds up at her.

At last with a snort she shook herself, and dipped her lips to the cool, running water. As she lowered her head she saw the remains of the dress wrapped around her leg. She touched her wet, wounded ankle with her lips and smelled blood. She flung her head away from it and did not try to drink.

The horse in the gully was silent now. The horse in the creek stood still—a frozen statue. The creek gurgled its safe little sounds and cool water curled around her four rigid feet.

2

Noon of a Tornado Day

It was noon of the day of the tornado. Mark was down in the barnyard feeding potato peelings to old Colonel. Of course, Mark did not know that this was going to be the day of the tornado. Nobody knew that late in the afternoon a tornado would come rising in a black roar over the hill and fall on the helpless countryside.

No, this noon when Mark was with Colonel it was a day like any other day except that Colonel still lay in the gateway between the barnyard and the pasture. The old horse had lain there all night and all the day before.

This morning when Mark had watched his mother peel potatoes for a salad for the church supper, he had thought that if he fed the peelings to Colonel maybe it would give the old horse strength to get up again. If he could get up he could eat grass and get stronger. Then they'd go across the pasture to the high bank of catalpa trees. There was a water pipe sticking out of the bank that came from a spring. He would hold a pail under the end of the pipe and when it filled, Colonel could drink. Then he'd eat more grass and maybe stay up on his feet.

But this noon Colonel couldn't even lift his head to nibble the parings from the flat pan. Mark sat discouraged until he tried rubbing a piece of peeling into the side of Colonel's mouth. It worked! Colonel opened his big, yellow teeth, chewed and swallowed!

Mark was so busy feeding the peelings into Colonel's mouth that he didn't hear his dad drive up to the barn, but his father saw him and called out, "Mark, what the blazes are you doing?"

"Just feeding Colonel," Mark yelled. "He can't get up to eat grass."

Dad came down the path. "How long has this been going on?"

"All night and all day yesterday," Mark said. "This is the longest time he's lain still. He can't get up. I thought if I fed him these peelings they'd make him strong enough to lift his head so I could hold it up like I do when he goes down. With his head held up he can get on his feet again."

"You've been holding his head up so he can get on his feet?" Dad sounded scared. "Mark, that's dangerous."

"Oh, no, Dad," Mark explained. "Colonel knows what to do. He looks at me out of the corner of his eyes to tell me to get out of the way because he's going to heave himself up. He always staggers a little until he gets steady, then he looks back to tell me it's safe, so then I take the rope on his halter and we go to the spring so he can drink. After that he's steady enough to eat grass. Sometimes he's steady enough that we go back to the woodlot so he can stand in the creek and cool his feet."

Dad stood shaking his head. "Promise me," he said, "promise me that you'll never do that again—never. At least not unless your mother is with you."

Mark looked up but he didn't promise. Dad just didn't know. But he and Colonel knew. Colonel always looked out for him. Colonel was his friend.

Dad studied Colonel and shook his head.

"Guess I've been so busy finishing that new store in Stanton that I haven't paid much attention to what's going on around here. I didn't realize it had got this bad with the old horse." Dad pressed his lips together. At last he said, "Mark, this oughtn't to come as a surprise to you—you were with me when I bought this farm. All I wanted was the wonderful old house, but the farmer wouldn't sell it. No, I had to take the farm and the old horse with it. The old man was getting ready to go into a home but first he had to see that the old horse was provided for. You remember that, don't you?"

Remember? He remembered every word. "No, you can't have the house unless you take the farm and the horse," the old man had told Dad. "He's on his last legs, that horse. It won't be long. But he was born on this farm and he's going to die on it. He deserves that much."

When the farmer had said that, Mark had pulled at his dad's arm, "Dad! Dad! Please buy him. I'll take care of him. Can he be mine— can he?"

The farmer had answered for Dad. "Yes, boy. If your dad buys the farm, Colonel will be yours. See that you take good care of him."

"Oh, I will, I will," Mark had promised. Then he hadn't listened to anything else. He'd run over to stand close to the horse that was going to be his. The man had said so!

Now Dad stood shaking his head. He bent to look closely at Colonel. "Remember, the old man told us Colonel was on his last legs? He *is* on his last legs now, Mark, and you've got to face it."

Mark got up and stood stiff and straight. You didn't cry before your dad—but you wanted to. Dad kept talking.

"Can't you understand that to keep Colonel like this is cruel? We promised the old man that we'd give the horse the best of care. This isn't the best, it's the worst—lying here hungry and thirsty and too weak to get up. I'll go over to the Home and tell the old man first but I know he'll agree it's the only thing to do. Mark, the Vet will put Colonel out of his misery and it'll be quick and easy—it'll be a mercy for the poor old fellow."

Mark looked up at Dad. He couldn't believe it. How could grown-ups make themselves believe things just by saying them?

How could Dad say it?

How could he believe it?

Why would it be a mercy—Colonel'd be dead, wouldn't he?

"Mark, tomorrow's your birthday, isn't it?"

Mark nodded. He didn't dare to speak, or he'd cry.

"Well, then, how'd you like a pony?" Dad looked around the pasture. "What an ocean of grass! Maybe we ought to get a whale—still, whales don't swim so good in grass. Well, how *about* a pony?"

It was hard to keep the tears back with Dad making unfunny jokes. He didn't want a pony. He had Colonel and Colonel was his friend. Why couldn't Dad understand? He shook his head.

"Well . . . maybe your mother can explain it better." Dad started toward the house.

Now there was nothing to do but crouch down and start feeding Colonel again.

Finally dad came out of the house and went to the barn. He called down, "Okay, Mark. Your mother says to give Colonel a little longer. She says maybe he'll get up for your birthday tomorrow. If I find time this afternoon I might be able to look for a young horse or a pony. Maybe with a young horse on the place Colonel will want to be young again. Who knows . . ."

"Dad! Dad!" Mark shouted, "If it made Colonel stay on his feet then I'd have two horses and then . . ."

But Dad had started the truck and the whole barn roared with the noise. Colonel lifted his head at the sudden roar. Then Mark couldn't just stand there yelling—Colonel had his head up, Colonel could drink.

Mark stormed across the pasture to fill a pail from the spring. When he got back Colonel still had his head up enough to drink out of the tipped-down pail. It was sloshy, but Colonel did drink. After that Mark got busy. He found an old rusty sickle in the barn and a bushel basket. He went behind the house where the grass grew the greenest and the juiciest in the shade from the cellarway's propped-up door. He cut a whole basketful and carried it to Colonel. Then he folded it in little bundles and shoved the bundles between Colonel's teeth down into his mouth. Colonel's yellow old teeth got green-juicy from the tender grass. Oh, it must be full of strength and goodness. It had to get Colonel back on his feet—if not today then tomorrow.

When Mother called Mark for lunch, Colonel still wasn't up. He'd had two bushels of

grass and the potato peelings but he hadn't
even tried to get up. Maybe he was saving his
strength so he could get up tomorrow, but it
wasn't easy to make yourself believe it. So it
wasn't easy to eat lunch with Mother in the
quiet kitchen. Mother made a little joke too.
She asked, "What do you want for your birthday—a bushel of oats for Colonel?"

He didn't feel like joking—but a bushel of
oats! There ought to be all kinds of strength in
a bushel of oats. So he said, "Yes, if you're not
joking, I would like that." He had to say it
slowly or he'd start to cry.

But Mother said, "Okay then, it'll be one of
your presents but I'll get it today. Now that
your dad came home to get the truck and left
the car here I'm going to go into the city for
some shopping, but on the way home I'll stop
at the feed mill for the oats and maybe a tonic
—if they have a tonic for horses. But look,
whose birthday is this, yours or Colonel's?
Anyhow, I've got a present right now for your
horse. When I was peeling potatoes for the
salad, I cut up all the small ones I found into
tiny pieces so they won't choke Colonel. You
can give them to him after lunch."

Suddenly Mark was afraid. He wanted to

ask, Mother, why are you giving Colonel presents? Do you know he is going to die?

But he couldn't ask it. That would make it real. "May I go out and feed him now?" he asked instead.

"Yes, but don't spend the whole afternoon with Colonel. Play a little and let Colonel rest."

He was almost at the door when he put down the pail and rushed back to kiss Mother hard. Then he promised, "I'll play in the tunnels I made in the hay pile in the barn. I'll play a long time."

He was going to do it, too. It would be a kind of bargain. He'd feed Colonel, maybe give him another drink and then he wouldn't even go near him. He wouldn't cheat by watching through the cracks of the barn up in the haymow to see if Colonel *had* got up on his feet. He'd play almost the whole afternoon. That would be *his* part of the bargain. Then if he kept his part Colonel would live. It had to be.

"Mark," Mother called from the kitchen door, "feed Colonel the potatoes but don't expect them to change into strength just like that —it takes a while. You play and let Colonel rest after the potatoes, then maybe by the time your dad comes home Colonel will have strength enough so that Dad and I can help you get him up on his feet."

That was a wonderful thought. Mark stopped and looked back but he was too taken up with it to answer.

"And Mark, your dad wants to go out to that pony farm to see just what they have. He doesn't know what they cost, but he'd feel better if you had a pony. You think about it while you play."

Mark nodded. He didn't answer because he didn't know—he didn't want anything but Colonel. He'd think about it, but later.

"See you, Mom, see you," he yelled as he ran toward the barnyard.

3

The Bargain

Mark lay stretched out in his new, partly dug tunnel under the hay pile up in the barn. He'd had to stop digging because the fine hay dust was making him sneeze. He had his face in his arms waiting for the last sneeze when the question jumped into his mind—would it be nice to have a pony? A pony would be his size. He could ride a pony. He wouldn't have to claw himself up the way he did with Colonel. He only got up on Colonel when the old horse wasn't lame and stumbly, but he was always sorry when he did. Colonel was a big old work horse, bony and wide. He had to sit spraddled, legs sticking out straight, and it hurt. Riding Colonel was like riding a bony earthquake. Mark laughed—Colonel a bony earthquake!

It was easier and more fun just to walk with

Colonel. But now he had shown Colonel all the spots that he knew over the whole farm—even small bird nests hidden down in the grass. That was important so that during school when Colonel was grazing alone he wouldn't crush the nests with his big, flat, squashed-out feet.

But Colonel knew all kinds of places too. Colonel had been born on this farm. He knew. He was the one who had shown Mark the little whispering creek that ran through the gully and on through the woodlot. When you stood still under the trees it was hushed and important. It was almost like being in church except that the little creek always whispered. It was so narrow they couldn't wade together, so Mark had to come splashing on behind Colonel. But often Colonel just wanted to stand with the creek water washing and whispering around his feet. What if Colonel had got up from all the strength of the pail full of potatoes—what if he was up right now! Then they could go to the cool-water creek in the woodlot under the trees.

But Mark did not push back out of his stifling tunnel. He'd promised Mother and he'd made a bargain so he was going to play here in the hay pile. Somehow he felt sure that if he did everything right and was obedient it would help Colonel. Mark began tunneling again—it was hot and dusty and sneezy under the hay, but it was the only way he knew of keeping himself from sneaking looks at Colonel. Then suddenly he broke through into the main tunnel that he'd made long ago. He'd done it, he'd played and he'd broken through.

He'd played just as he'd promised, and he'd kept his part of the bargain. But a pony wouldn't be any good.

Mark lay panting after crawling into the main tunnel. There was light at the end of this tunnel, dim barn light, and there was air. It was even a little cooler here—but not much.

Colonel must be hot in the barnyard right in the sun. Oh, it was still, lonely and still. Man, he felt hot and thirsty. Colonel must be thirsty too, out there in the sun and after that whole pan of potatoes. If Colonel needed a pailful of water it wouldn't be cheating to get him a drink. And then if Colonel could lift his head that high to drink out of the pail—of course he'd have to hold Colonel's head up—why, then what if Colonel came up on his feet? There he'd be on his feet when Mother and

Dad came home, and nothing to do but feed him oats, and big spoonfuls of tonic.

What time was it anyhow? The light looked sort of dim. It could be late. He'd played and played and thought and thought and it had taken a long time to feed the potatoes to Colonel. What if right now Dad and Mother were on their way home? And Colonel still down because he needed water. He'd run to the house and look at the clock and if there was time he'd get a pail of water for Colonel.

Mark scrambled down the haymow ladder and stopped startled in the open doorway of the barn. It wasn't only the barn that was dim! Everything everywhere was dim and mean and threatening. Everything was waiting. Had he really played so long under the hay that it was late? But Mother and Dad still weren't home. Mark flew to the house to look at the clock.

Oh, it *was* late, way late—ten to six. Much later than Dad usually came home. There wouldn't be time to run to the spring. He looked out of the window and saw that Colonel was still down—flat down. He'd looked, but it was late—he'd kept his part of the bargain!

Mark ran to the living room where he could

see far down the road, but there was no car coming. Mark fretted at the window. Maybe they were so late because they'd gone to get a pony. What could he do if they came with a pony? You couldn't tell your parents, "No, I don't want it for my birthday." Not if it was here.

Mark moved along the windows until at the dining room window he could look across the single field that separated their farm from the Sayers farm. As Mark stood there Mr. and Mrs. Sayers came running out of their house. Mr. Sayers was carrying a radio but Mrs. Sayers stood looking toward their house as if looking straight at him.

Then they looked up at the sky and Mr. Sayers ran back and grabbed Mrs. Sayers' arm and started tugging her out toward their barn. But as if she had seen Mark at the window she pulled away from her husband and seemed to be shouting. Mark couldn't hear because there came a great roaring. He ran out of the house and into the field but Mr. Sayers motioned him back with the waving radio. Mrs. Sayers screamed and screamed at him but he couldn't make out a word for the awfulness of the roaring.

Then Mr. Sayers pointed and Mark looked up. Over the hill came a great black cloud, swinging and threatening. Then Mrs. Sayers' scream pierced through the noise. "Mark, get into the basement—it's a tornado!"

Mark ran toward the barn. "Not in your barn, not in your barn!" Mrs. Sayers yelled. But now the two old people were running to their barn—funny, he wasn't to run to his!

"Colonel is down, I've got to . . ." Mark screamed down the field. But the old people couldn't hear, they kept running, already the tornado was there behind them. It twisted and whirled in the sky and then it dipped down on their house. Immediately it rose again, but now there was no roof on the house. Only the roofless walls were left under the screaming blackness.

Confused, scared, threatened, Mark started to run to Colonel but suddenly there was such a wrenching, screeching noise, Mark turned and stood rooted. It was the Sayers' barn! The tornado had the barn and now it rose up with it, and there were only the bare basement walls left. The tornado had the barn and Mr. and Mrs. Sayers must be up in the tornado.

Now the tornado turned toward the single

field that was between their houses—now it was coming for him and he couldn't move! He couldn't move and there lay Colonel!

He heard himself screeching, "Run, Colonel. Run!" Colonel couldn't run but somehow it helped him to move. Then he was at the cellarway with the open trap door. There was nothing he could do for Colonel now. He hurled himself down the steps.

Now the tornado would get Colonel. Mark rushed up the steps again—if he could get Colonel up and in the basement of the barn with him. . . .

There wasn't time. The tornado had already crossed the field. It was in the yard, and the cellar door was still open. Mark unhooked the door and tried to pull it down over him but the tornado was so close the suction flapped the door up and flapped the door down like a great wooden wing. There Mark hung, unable to let go. There he hung watching Colonel, listening to Colonel's screaming. The old horse's scream was so scared and so shrill that it cut through the roar of the tornado.

Then Colonel flung his head back so far that Mark saw Colonel's head upside down, his screaming mouth open and his big teeth showing. In a mighty lunge he rolled over, gathered his legs under him and was up. He staggered only a moment, then with great stiff plunges he tore into the pasture ahead of the tornado. Colonel was up! The next moment the slinging cloud of blackness closed in behind him and Mark could see him no more.

The suction suddenly was gone. The trap door fell shut with a slap like thunder. It smashed Mark down the steps. He rolled limply along the scattered potatoes. Everything went black and still.

4

Horse in the Creek

It was as if by inches Mark came back to consciousness. His cheek and nose were against something soft and cushiony that had a musty, earthy smell. He took it in his hand—it was a potato, it squashed. "Mom! Dad!" he screamed. No one answered, everything was still. Mark scrambled to his feet. He was dizzy but now he knew where he was, now he remembered. But everything was still, too still.

He was in the cellar. He'd been lying among the potatoes where the trap door had flung him when it had crashed down. There had been a tornado and from the cellar door he had seen Colonel get to his feet and gallop into the pasture ahead of the tornado.

Now in one mighty slam the stillness was broken. Rain thundered on the closed trap door and found cracks in the splintered, rotted wood. Big drops smacked against Mark's neck and crawled coldly down his back. With one hand Mark felt the top of his head where the door had hit and where the slow blood throbbed. His head was wet, but rain-wet, not blood-wet—blood would be warm and sticky. This was cold and crawly with crumbles and splinters of wood. He queasily wiped out his neck with the flat of his hand, and staggered up the cellar steps. He had to get outside and see what had happened to Colonel.

Mark braced himself, both hands around the edge of the top step and with bent back up against the soaked, warped door he tried to force it out of its framework. He heaved himself up against it but it did not yield. The rain was coming harder now. It soaked his head, ran down inside his shirt, divided and ran down both legs into his socks and his shoes. It was cold but it stopped the throbbing in his head. He stepped down to the middle step and let the rain water sluice over his head and wash down his face.

Suddenly he felt foolish. Here he was heaving away at a stuck door with his head pounding when all he had to do was to feel his way across the cellar and up the inside stairway to the dining room. He shuffled through the scattered potatoes so as not to fall again. Heck, he was a dirty, wet mess anyway! He dropped to his hands and knees and crawled up the inside stairway.

When Mark opened the door to the dining room he was startled to see that it was almost as dark up here as it had been in the windowless cellar. The whole house was enclosed in a dark curtain of rain. The gutters could not hold the smash of rain that thundered on the roof, they overflowed and the water spilled down in thick, dark sheets over the windows. Inside the house was empty and silent, except for him. Was it night-dark or rain-dark? How long had he lain in the cellar?

Mark ran to see the kitchen clock. The hands still stood at ten to six—right where they'd stood just before the tornado. Then must have been when the electric wires had gone down between here and Stanton.

He turned to snap on the light. There was no light. He lifted the receiver on the wall telephone above the kitchen table. The phone was as silent as the clock. The telephone wires were down, too.

Nobody would call—nobody could. And in a rain like this no one could come. Only night was coming—night and dark and rain. In such a rain not even Mr. Sayers could walk across the field that separated their houses and he couldn't get out to the neighbors. Oh! He'd forgotten! The neighbors were gone—gone with their barn. Colonel was gone. There was no one.

The thought of Colonel made Mark race to the storeroom that had its window above the cellar door. But he could only see as far as the barn and it was just a dull red lump inside the sheets of rain roaring off its roof. The barnyard sloping to the pasture was a boiling, racing river. Mark shivered. If Colonel hadn't gotten up, he would have drowned where he had lain. If it hadn't been for the tornado coming so close, Colonel wouldn't have gotten up.

If Colonel had fallen again, if he lay with his head to the ground, he could die in the pasture. Mark couldn't see, he couldn't go out there, could he? If he fell in the dark, he'd drown too, wouldn't he? And a lantern wouldn't stay lit.

Lantern! Mark tore back to the kitchen,

jerked open the cabinet door under the sink and, as he'd remembered, there was the lantern. He shook it. Oil rattled. He lit the lantern and set it in the sink for safety.

When he'd done that there was nothing more to do but stand listening to the rain that closed everything out but closed him in. If Colonel was alive, the rain was beating down on him, even if he was up on his feet. It must hurt, it must feel like hail or sharp, beating sticks. But even that would be better than Colonel lying flat on the ground.

He would wait for the rain to slow down, but he'd get his boots and raincoat and have them ready. He ran to his room.

Back in the kitchen he pulled on his boots, then he thought of something else. Leaving his raincoat and hat on a chair he went gallumping in his clumsy boots to the storeroom, where he'd seen a big carton. He jumped on it and smashed it to flatness. The rain must be slowing, for his stamping had seemed noisier than the rain.

With the flattened carton Mark went back to the kitchen. He laid it on the table and hunted a carpenter's flat pencil out of the drawer—that would write thick and black.

He listened while he thought about what he should write. The rain must be slowing. Quickly he wrote: "Mom, Dad. The tornado came and Colonel got up and ran into the pasture. I couldn't help him then but now I have to find him. If I'm not here when you come I'm out looking for Colonel."

He'd made the writing good and big. He set the carton on the sink. The moment they opened the door they'd see it by lantern light. There was still a space at the bottom of the carton. He'd write small. "Mr. and Mrs. Sayers went up in the tornado with their barn." He put the carton back. Small as he'd written these last words, they seemed the biggest of all, they were so scary. He picked up the pencil and added: "I think." It was a little better, but not much. He set the coffee pot against the carton so it couldn't fall down on the lantern. Then he pulled the window curtain to one side to see if the rain was stopping.

It had slowed. The water wasn't gushing over the edge of the gutter anymore, and across the field a queer evening light had come into the sky. It showed the white walls of the Sayers' house standing open to the rain. The rain fell dark inside the white walls. Their barn was gone, the old people were gone and suddenly Mark noticed that the old white car that had seldom run had also gone up in the tornado.

The strange light glistened on something in the road in front of the Sayers' house. It was a great roll and tangle of twisted, gleaming wires —the telephone and the electric wires rolled together and the dark wooden telephone poles rolled inside the wires.

There was no road to Stanton anymore. Beyond the wires the road ran dead into a mass of upended, uprooted trees. The roadside trees were smashed down in the road from both sides and other trees rose out of them as if planted upside down, their great stark roots upstanding. Under the trees the streaming road lay like a river.

Then the rain stopped. Now nothing but the water moved, and the queer, glassy light faded from the sky. Night darkness came to take the place of rain darkness. There was no sound except the drip, drip, drip.

Mark moved away from the window to his rain clothes. If he looked outside any longer, he'd be too scared to move. Mother and Dad couldn't come. There wasn't any road. If they walked, it would take them hours. But the pasture would be dark. Mark reached for the lantern. No, if he took it, and Mother and Dad did come, they wouldn't be able to read his note. And if he didn't find Colonel and had to come back alone, there wouldn't be any light in the window.

It was scary to go out and it was scary here. Mark pulled the rain hat down hard over his head. He was *going* to find Colonel! He'd bring him to the house, get the lantern and then be with Colonel and the lantern in the big, safe barn.

Mark threw the back door open and ran out, letting it slam shut behind him. It sounded like a shot as he raced away.

He made loud, splashy sounds with his boots in the water. He stamped so hard that the water splashed cold up his pants legs under his raincoat. It was shivery but the loud sounds helped. He ran around the barn by the high side to the open doors. The water would be too deep in the sunken barnyard to go by way of the pasture gate as Colonel had done.

It wasn't raining anymore and he didn't need his raincoat, he was wet anyway. He ripped it off as he ran and flung it toward the open doors. It'd be hard enough to climb the fence in his clumsy boots without having the raincoat in his way.

Without the raincoat Mark felt freed and speedy. He must hurry. Suddenly he realized he was in the pasture. There'd been no fence to climb. It was gone—ripped away where it had been nailed to the corner of the barn!

Mark stared. The tornado had come around the barn that close! It had ripped the fence away as if the quicker to get at Colonel. It had been that low to the ground. But when he'd seen it beyond the barn, it had been high enough that he'd seen Colonel plunge out ahead of it. If it had been low, he couldn't have seen Colonel. That meant the tornado had been lifting up into the sky. It couldn't have sucked Colonel up, could it?

It was only when the tornado came down over things like it did over the Sayers' barn that it whirled them up into itself. If it was already high in the sky, Colonel would have been safe. He must be somewhere in the pasture.

Mark felt easier. He yelled Colonel's name out ahead of him as he ran. Now his eyes were more accustomed to the faint light and he could run faster. But suddenly in the midst of a running step Mark stopped cold. He backed away a little and couldn't force himself on. Colonel wasn't safe at all. He couldn't be! The middle pasture was full of big, heavy things. The tornado had dumped stuff everywhere. The pasture was crazy with things that belonged in people's houses—not in a field! There was a white enamel stove in the grass with a mirror smashed into it. Far away small starlight trembled in the broken slivers. There were beds and tables and a smashed dresser and doors driven into the ground among big beams from barns speared down into the grass. And there lay a kitchen sink. Some of it must have hit Colonel.

And there beyond the clutter of mixed-up things was a roof—a whole roof in their pasture. It was the roof of the Sayers' house! It was the scariest of all, the roof of a house you *knew* in your pasture. Suppose that roof had come down on Colonel! The tornado hadn't sucked Colonel up but it must have hurled everything at the galloping horse. Maybe right now Colonel lay smashed under the roof, maybe he was hurt, maybe Colonel was needing him.

A whimper in his throat, Mark raced down the pasture to the roof. Halfway there his legs bounced up from under him and he was thrown flat. He'd run across a soggy mattress in the grass. Lying flat, Mark saw just beyond him a big roll of money with a rubber band around it. He crawled over and picked it up. Working the wet money into his pocket, looking down at it, made it easier to get to the roof. Colonel wasn't there. In his relief Mark all but danced up the slant of the roof, over the shingles to the ridge. From there he could pick out details in the pasture clear to the deep gully that separated it from the woodlot beyond. There were more stars now, with more light. Why, everything was clear and clean at the pasture's end.

The smashed-down junk was only in the middle pasture. Nowhere lay the white of Colonel, but neither was Colonel standing in the clean end of the pasture. Then it must be that Colonel had gone to stand in the creek with his sore feet. He always did.

Mark yelled, "Colonel," and ran down the steep slope of the roof, and with that start he galloped to the pasture's end by the gully.

The tornado had been in the gully! Down

there lay twisted trees in a tangle of ghost-white roots.

But something whiter than the roots was among the tangle of leaves and branches. In the gully under the torn-up trees was the white of Colonel.

It wasn't fair! Whole big trees had come down on Colonel. The tornado hadn't taken him up, the tornado hadn't smashed the tables and stoves down on him, but just before old Colonel could get to his creek in the woodlot, the tornado had smashed him down with trees. Mark couldn't move. He couldn't believe it. He'd kept his part of the bargain. It wasn't fair!

Then suddenly he knew—it couldn't be the white of Colonel. He knew, now he *knew* it was the chalky white of Mr. Sayers' old-fashioned car. That's what it was. Why, Colonel couldn't even get down the steep side of the gully. He'd been so worried about Colonel that he'd thought everything white must be Colonel.

Mark turned and ran along the gully's high bank, down the long slope to the woodlot. That's where Colonel would be—cooling his feet in the creek water.

And as he ran in under the dark trees of the woodlot, there *was* a horse in the creek. But it was a dark horse. Uneasily Mark inched forward. In the hushed darkness under the big trees the little creek went on whispering. Mark had a strange thought. This morning Dad had talked about another horse. Could this be the birthday horse? Could Dad have brought this horse to the woodlot to keep it secret until tomorrow, his birthday? It was so solemn and quiet here with the drip of the trees and the creek's whispering that it was easy to believe anything. The horse did not look up.

He couldn't find Colonel. He'd looked everywhere. He was going to bring this horse to the barn. It wouldn't be so alone. He'd believe the was his horse until Dad told him differently.

Mark edged forward to look at the horse. She was a beauty. She was sleek and lean and brown. She was slim and young. "I'm going to call you 'Creek,'" he told her, "because you are here in Colonel's creek. I'm going to take you home and call you Creek while I have you."

Mark's soft whispering made the new horse look up at him and just then, just as Creek looked up, a horse neighed. The neighing came from the gully. Colonel *was* in the gully, Colonel was alive!

"Colonel! Colonel!" Mark screamed, "I'm coming, I'm coming!"

His yeling made the new horse rear and tremble. "Aw, I scared you," Mark said. "That's from being in the tornado, isn't it?" He stood wavering, anxious to rush to Colonel, but needing to quiet the new horse. She shook and put her head down. Mark saw the piece of dress wrapped around her ankle. A loose end of the stuff floated in the creek's current. That was what was making her nervous. He'd take it off before he ran to Colonel. He slid down the bank into the creek and rapped on the horse's leg to indicate she was to lift her hoof. He began to unwrap the flimsy cloth.

Oh, but it wasn't just a piece of dress—it was a bandage. There was blood. The bandage mustn't come off. Mark wrapped it around the ankle again and puzzled how to keep it in place in the running water. The horse looked down at him. Mark wrenched the roll of bills out of his pocket and stripped off the rubber band. "Golly, I just remembered this money. Look, it's got a rubber band. That'll hold your bandage, that'll fix it."

The horse seemed to understand. It was simple to secure the bandage with the rubber band. Far simpler than getting the wet money back in his pocket. In his impatience to get to Colonel, Mark dropped the money. He pounced and grabbed most of the bills before they floated away in the current, shoved them in his pocket and clambered up out of the creek. "I'm going to get Colonel," he told the new horse. "You just wait here. We'll be right back."

Mark kept looking back over his shoulder to be sure the new horse was all right as he hurried away. Then the new horse threw up her head and whinnied after him.

As if it were an echo, there came an answering whinny out of the gully. "Hear?" Mark called back. "That's Colonel."

Now, there was nothing scary about the gully with its ghostly, uprooted trees in the dark night.

It was marvelous how Colonel had done it. He must have run down the steep side of the gully into the snarl of trees right after they'd been turned upside down by the tornado. He'd run into the great V crotch of the biggest tree of all. The man-thick branches of the big crotch had squeezed Colonel in, and held him up on his stiff old legs. Then the small branches had snapped back in place under him. There he stood in a prison of branches that kept him on his feet.

"Oh, you," he praised Colonel. "Oh, you were smart." But Colonel didn't like his prison. He whinnied over Mark's head toward the creek. Then he looked down and his long underlip quivered and flopped. He didn't have a bit of patience with Mark being so slow in freeing him. Well, of course not. Colonel wanted to see the new horse who would be his mate—if she stayed, if he could keep her. It was a wonderful thought.

"She's a she," Mark told Colonel while he tugged and bent back the thicker branches. With them out of the way Colonel backed out of the crotch and just waded down the smaller branches. He crushed them.

Once out of the crotch, Colonel wheeled and made straight for the woodlot. Mark had to run to catch the rope on Colonel's halter. Colonel went straight for the new horse.

The two horses didn't neigh, didn't nuzzle, but they crowded so close together that their whole sides touched. They must be sending messages through their skins, because slowly all the shakes and shivers went out of Creek and she stood quiet and slim beside thick old Colonel.

Everything was so still that Mark could hear the creek making its soft whisperings. Now he had Colonel back and now he knew how to keep him up on his feet. All Colonel needed was something under him so he couldn't lie down on his stiff, sore legs.

Would that be a big surprise for Dad! If he could fix up Colonel's stall in the barn to show Dad how Colonel could be kept on his feet, then the old horse could stay on the farm. And now—at least for a while—there would be Creek. Colonel and Creek! Creek and Colonel! Mark's tongue fondled the names. And suppose things turned out that Creek could stay, oh, it would be wonderful.

Mark couldn't wait to try out his plan. He grabbed the rope of Colonel's halter and led him through the water to the end of the wood-lot. The new horse followed sweetly down the narrow, winding creek.

The tornado had tossed everything into the middle pasture, but the lane that led to the barn lay neat and clear. The horses could walk side by side and Mark walked between them. The hoofs of the horses thudded on the springy sod. Their big bodies made inside sounds and outside creakings as they swayed and swung along. Colonel walked just as long-legged as Creek to keep up with her—as if she were his wife. Mark laughed out exultantly and walked straight, tall and sure between their bobbing heads. He wasn't coming home alone at all. And Colonel had a wife, and he a new friend. Most of all he had Colonel back safe. Dad would see what wonderful things Creek was doing for Colonel. Oh, Dad had been right— Creek was making Colonel young.

5

Milk Wagon Ambulance

As Mark walked down the lane between his two horses and the big barn loomed near, he couldn't make up his mind. He did so want his parents to be home when he came with the horses, yet he wanted to have Colonel all fixed in his stall so Dad could see how Colonel could be kept on his feet. Colonel walked fine now, just as fast as Creek. And after lying all that time in the barnyard. It must be that the hard, fast run to get away from the tornado had unlimbered his stiff old legs. He'd even plunged down the steep side of the gully.

Mark glanced down at the dress wrapped around Creek's leg. In a way it made Creek more Colonel's wife—she with one bad leg and Colonel with four—it made them belong together.

Mark felt that since such wonderful things had happened—Colonel alive and Creek coming—another wonderful thing should happen too. Just as soon as he came around the barn the headlights of Dad's truck should shine on him and his two horses. Mother and Dad would look down through the big windshield and hardly believe what they saw.

What if it would happen? It could! Maybe Dad's truck could have come through the fields even though the roads were blocked. Now in a minute they'd be around the barn!

If the truck was there, he'd stand right in the glare of the headlights and the minute Dad jumped down he'd say, "Dad, see my family of horses? Colonel got up on his feet and Creek came to be Colonel's wife. You did get her for my birthday, didn't you? But if you didn't, can we still keep her?"

But no truck was there and nothing was coming—no headlights, no rumble of a truck. Mark was disappointed but he stood there thinking. Mr. and Mrs. Sayers had gone up with *their* barn in the tornado—maybe the owners of Creek had gone in the tornado too. Then there'd be no one but him to take care of Creek—feed her, fix her ankle and be her friend. Oh, if Creek could stay.

Mark looked toward the house. It rose dark against the faint sky light with only a dim gleam from the lantern in the kitchen sink. There was no truck behind the house. He looked in the doors of the upper barn. There was only his raincoat where he'd flung it on the ramp. He looked across the dark field where the Sayers house stood roofless, without any light, without any people. Even their big barn gone. He shivered. The long, black night was here. He moved closer to Colonel.

"Come," he said, "I'm going to get the lantern and fix your stall for you." The two horses followed him to the kitchen door. He gave Colonel a pat on the shoulder, "Keep Creek with you," he said. He ran in, grabbed the lantern, ran back to the horses and they followed him willingly to the barn.

Inside, Mark puzzled where to keep the horses while he worked on Colonel's stall. Colonel mustn't lie down or he wouldn't be able to get up again. Then in the far corner Mark saw the little old-fashioned milk wagon that had belonged to the old man who had owned the farm. He tied Creek and Colonel side by side to one of the wheels. Now Colonel would be safe.

Now what to use to hold Colonel up? There

had to be something, there was so much stuff the old man had left. Then as Mark searched he spied it. Up on a cross beam lay a thick roll of something that looked heavy enough. He poked it down with a stick. It unrolled over the floor, broad and thick and webbed. Mark lifted an end—it was tough and strong. It would be just right. It was long enough that he could cut it in sections and have two or three heavy pieces to go under Colonel's thick old body to keep him up. If he nailed the ends of the belts to the wall above Colonel's stall, put Colonel in the stall, looped the belts under him and then up and over the other side of the wall and nailed them with big spikes, Colonel couldn't possibly weigh them down. He'd just rest on them—even sleep, sleep without lying down.

Mark stormed to the tool box, found spikes and a hammer and a sickle knife. Then he took a barrel, rolled it into Colonel's stall, set it up. He cut the belt in three pieces, climbed on the barrel and nailed the belt to the wall. He hung from it to test it—it was strong and the three spikes held it secure. He jumped down hanging on to the belt. The mighty jerk almost pulled his arms from their sockets but the broad belt held tight.

Mark took the other two lengths and nailed them beside the first one. Then he had to lead Colonel away from Creek. "It's just for a few moments," he told her, "then I'll tie you to Colonel's crib and even though you'll be on the other side of the partition you can see each other and you can eat hay out of the crib with Colonel . . . and Mother is going to bring oats," he promised. Creek needed to be near Colonel after what the tornado had done to her. Alone she was shaky.

It wasn't as easy and fast as he'd promised himself and Creek. He had to hang from the first belt to draw it snug and tight under Colonel's body and hold it that way, and at the same time push a spike into the webbing of the belt and hammer it down. The first nail spat across the barn and tinkled away over the concrete floor. Creek jumped and tugged at her rope until the little milk wagon wheels screaked.

It was such a high, squealy noise that Mark twisted around on top of the barrel. But there had also been a sound—as if someone was pounding on the ramp of the upper barn, as if someone had come running through the doorway above and then had run right down the ramp again. Mark stared up at the rafters—he didn't know, he'd been so intent on his job and on Creek that it was as if he hadn't heard the pounding until it was over. It must have been the wagon Creek had dragged across the floor.

He nailed two more spikes in the belt and then he stopped. Could it have been Dad? What if it had been and there lay his raincoat? Dad wouldn't know what to make of it.

"Colonel," Mark begged, "don't lie down." He jumped down from the barrel. "I'll be right back, maybe with Dad."

But when Mark ran out of the basement and around to the upper barn he could see that the house was dark. There was no sound. There seemed to be no one. But when he dashed up the ramp there was no raincoat lying there. Someone or something had taken his raincoat!

Mark stood staring at the house and as he stared a ray from a flashlight ranged through the kitchen.

"Dad!" Mark screamed. "Dad! Mother!"

The light stabbed out of the kitchen door and picked him out as he came running.

"Mark, boy!" a voice yelled. "Mark. Thank God you're alive."

But it wasn't Dad. It was Mr. Sayers.

"Mr. Sayers! I saw your barn go up—how did you get away from the tornado?"

"We didn't. It took the whole barn—and left nothing but us and the grain bin."

Mr. Sayers opened the screen door to let Mark in. They stood looking at each other and then the old man said, "Son, I've got to sit down—let's sit down together." They went into the living room by the light of the flashlight and sat on the sofa. But for a while Mr. Sayers did not talk, then he said slowly, "This flashlight's all I've got. We'd best talk in the dark."

"I've got a lantern in the barn but it's almost out of oil." Mark said.

Then the old man roused himself. "Mark, your mother talked over the radio. There's no way for her to get out here. So she asked anybody that could—especially me—to come and look after you."

"But Mother was coming home with Dad from Stanton and maybe he was bringing a pony on his truck."

"Listen, Mark. Stanton is nearly all gone in the tornado. It went right through the village and your dad got hurt—how, I don't know.

51

All I know is that they got him into the hospital in the city and your mother's with him."

"Is he hurt bad?" Mark's voice was shaky.

"All I know is what I've told you, son. He's alive and in the hospital. That's something this night. Mama's hurt bad, and she's lying in our dusty old oat bin. It's all that's left of our barn. If that danged old tornado hadn't taken my old car, too, I'd have tried to get her in to the hospital in it—but the roads are blocked."

Mark jumped up. "Look, Mr. Sayers. There's an old milk wagon in our barn and a new horse that came in the tornado, her leg is cut but maybe she could pull the milk wagon and there's the road behind our farm that Dad sometimes comes down with the truck— maybe we could go to the hospital that way and maybe there'd be a house with a telephone and we could call the hospital for Mrs. Sayers and talk to Mother."

"Boy, boy! It just could be—it's got to be! Help me get a mattress from one of your beds to put in the back of the wagon." He shoved the flashlight at Mark. "Show me the way."

"Creek's leg is bad—that's the horse that came here—so I don't know for sure she can pull a wagon."

"Everything's hurt tonight," Mr. Sayers

said. "And if she could run here . . . well, anyhow what's least hurt has got to help what's really hurt. I'll look at the leg."

They ripped the bedding off Mark's bed and let it heap on the floor. "You can run back for that while I look at the horse," the old man said.

They set the mattress straight up. Mr. Sayers draped the mattress cover over the edge. "We'll take it, too. I can rip it up for bandages —it's as thick as canvas. It'll hold the cut together."

They slid the mattress down the stairs, then hoisted it under their arms. In the barn the lantern was still burning. They shoved the mattress into the milk cart. It fit.

The old man was amazed at the broad belts under Colonel. Mark explained and the old man muttered, "An old threshing-machine belt! Who but a kid would think of that?"

"But won't it work?" Mark asked anxiously.

"No reason why not. I'll help you nail up the other belts the moment we get the new horse fixed up. Now you run and get that bedding so we can tuck Mama in on the mattress. You take the flash. I can work on the horse by the lantern light."

When Mark got back with the bedding

Creek's leg was bound up tight with a strip of the mattress cover. "It's a deep, bad cut, and I suspect only a tornado kept her running on it—the dress wrapped around it helped. It may get worse if we use her on the wagon . . . we might ruin this horse, Mark. But it's got to be. Mama's got to get to the hospital and you've got to know about your dad. You understand?"

"Yes," Mark said with tight lips.

"Then run as fast as you can and tell Mama. She's in the grain bin and the door is closed—she can't get up. You just go right in. There's nothing left on her but her corset and some heaped-up oats, but don't let it bother you—that's the kind of night this is. Run now and stay with Mama while I cut down this old harness to Creek's size. No! I won't forget to nail the belts for Colonel. Go on, but take the flashlight."

Mark ran.

6

Grain Bin Hospital

Mark ran across the single field, squashing through the soggy grass, all the way to the roofless white house and the gone barn behind it. He did not use the flashlight clutched in his hand, he did not need it, he'd been in the dark so long with Colonel and Creek his eyes were night eyes now, like an owl's, like a cat's.

Mark slowed before the grimness of the concrete walls of the blown-away barn, stood in the empty doorway irresolute, then almost tiptoed across the tornado-scrubbed floor to the only thing left—the wooden-walled, wooden-roofed grain bin. The bin had a carpet draped over its top. He didn't know what to do, how to go about it. Mark knocked timidly on the closed door. Nobody answered. "Mama?" Mark called softly. Mr. Sayers called her "Mama," and saying "Mama," it would sound to her like somebody she knew.

First there was silence, then came a groan and then Mrs. Sayers called out: "Mark? Mark?" Her voice came the way his glad shout had come there in the woodlot: "Colonel! Colonel, alive!"

"Yes, it's me, Mark." Mark tugged at the door.

"No, don't come in just yet. Wait till I get some oats over me. Oh, Mark, safe and alive! If I could only scream it out so your mother could hear! Mark," Mama now said in a new voice, "run to the house and find me a dress in our upstairs bedroom closet. These oats keep running off me, and all the tornado left me was my corset. I'll bury down in the oats, and then you can bring my dress in to me."

Mark didn't tell her that their whole house roof was gone. He ran.

There was nothing in the whole upstairs, except rain water standing on the floors. There were no clothes in any closet, because nothing had a ceiling anymore—just the open, black air and starlight.

Down in the kitchen Mark rummaged through cabinet drawers and found one drawer full of towels, and, since they were all that was something like clothing, he pulled out the whole drawer and ran with it back to the grain bin.

Mama heard him. "You can come in, I'm buried somewhat now."

Mark climbed a box beside Mama's high grain bin bed so he could lift the drawer over to her. "I brought towels. Mama, there's nothing upstairs, the roof is gone and everything."

"Everything out of the closets too?" Mama asked sharply.

"Everything. The towels down in the kitchen were the only thing I could find. Will they help?"

As Mark lifted the drawer down to her, the oats shifted from under the heavy old woman and her legs shot up from under the oats. She grabbed a big towel and with one quick flick flapped it out open and over herself. "There, now it's all right, child. This is as decent as I can be."

But it wasn't all right, it was awful—Mark had seen. Her legs were all black and blue, and dirty and swollen, and her bare arms too.

Mama rested one elbow in the drawer and looked at her arm. "Like so much raw meat," she said bitterly. "Like so much raw, dirty meat. Child, when the tornado lifted the barn from over us, it swirled me flat on my face and flat on my back everywhichway all over the concrete floor. But I guess I was too heavy even for the tornado, although it ripped everything away but my corset. Then somehow Grandpa got to me and hung on to me, and when that awful sucking wind was gone, he dragged me to this bin and somehow hoisted me in here. And here's what's left of me, me and my corset."

"But we're going to take you to the hospital in the milk wagon in our barn. And, Mama, a horse came, and we can take you. Mr. Sayers is cutting down a harness, because Creek— that's the horse that came—is so slim. She's a riding horse, but she'll pull the wagon, and when we get to that road behind our farms, we'll call the hospital, and call Mother and talk to her, and everything . . . and everything will be fine."

The old woman listened, but dug and grabbled in the drawer all the while. Then she pulled out a card of safety pins and held them up triumphantly. "I thought so," she said. "In nearly every drawer all over the house I keep cards of safety pins—isn't that clever of me?" But a moan escaped her, and suddenly she lay out straight, crushing and wrenching the card of pins in her fist.

"So that's what he plans for me," she managed at last. "Well, I can tell him nobody puts me in any hospital as piggish dirty as I am. It's bad enough to come wrapped in towels."

She was trying to make a joke for him, Mark knew, but he had seen the awful thick legs with the bunched and lumped-out black veins, and all the skin scraped away. There was nothing to say, nothing to joke back.

"Don't hurt so for me, Mark," Mama said. "Listen now—we can do this. The old man will be busy a while if he's got to cut down a whole harness. You were in our kitchen—is the stove still there in one piece?"

Mark nodded.

"Then run and heat some water. It's an oil stove, and the matches are in the drawer above this towel drawer. We've got plenty of towels here, and pins. I'd be ashamed to come into a hospital dirty like this, it's bad enough coming diapered in towels. Run. Bring soap too. And a whole pailful of hot water."

The stove was whole, the stove would light, Mark rummaged in cabinets and found enough pans to put water heating on all the burners. It seemed ditheringly slow. Mr. Sayers wouldn't know what was happening here. Should he run and tell him? But Mr. Sayers would come, wouldn't he, the moment the harness was done and Creek was before the cart?

At last the water began its susurrusing sounds, and Mark turned off the burners and poured out the steaming water into one big pailful, and lugged it carefully to the barn. "I've got the water," he called out so Mama would know and be ready. He shoved the door open with his back and with his full pail climbed on the box. Mama lay on top of the oats now. She'd swaddle-diapered herself in the biggest towel, all tightly pinned, and had draped another towel over her shoulders like a shawl. She was tight-lipped from the effort. Mark lowered the pail and settled it in the oats and handed Mama the soap.

"Climb in here with me," Mama ordered. "I'll do my arms, but you wash the legs, I'm just too weak to sit up. You have to, Mark—a night like this you have to do strange things. Come on, boy, it's got to be." She soaped and wrung out a washcloth above the pail and handed it to him.

Mama started to wash her arm, but suddenly she just lay back. With the washcloth in one hand, the little flashlight in his mouth,

Mark timidly started to wash the old lady's leg, but at the first long soapy swipe the washcloth stopped.

"No, go on, boy," Mama ordered from between set lips. She was kneading her washcloth in her fist, with the other hand she'd grabbed the edge of the towel drawer and was lifting and wrenching it in her pain. "On with it—it's got to be."

"But it won't go!" Mark all but bawled out at her. "I didn't stop, the washcloth stopped. It's like washing a hedgehog. You're all over splinters. Mama, it's all tiny, fine splinters all over, and they catch in the washcloth—and everything's all puffed up and black and awful."

"I know, child. Don't I feel it? But that's why it's got to be cleaned, and that's why we've got to get to that hospital. They talked on the radio about gas gangrene. It comes with tornados. Fine splintery things, all dirty and messed, get driven down under your skin, and then comes gas gangrene. When Grandpa heard it, and nothing to be done, he got so scared, I sent him out to find you so I could lie here and groan all I wanted without it scaring the wits out of him. But I'm scared too, so it's got to be. But don't hurt so for me, child—I'll do the hurting, you do the washing. And don't look up here at me at all—don't mind if I blubber, it helps a little."

Flashlight in his mouth, Mark could not answer her, and it was as well, except that tears got in his eyes, and it was hard to swipe at them above the flashlight sticking out of his mouth. The sharp spot of light brought it all out—Mama's legs were a hedgehog of splinters, so fine, so thick, so many there was nowhere to begin. Mark dropped the washcloth and began picking again with both hands. It was an awful thought, and he was glad that with the flashlight in his mouth he couldn't blurt it out to Mama, but it was like plucking pin feathers out of a chicken, the way Mother often had him do because his fingers were small and quick. But pin feathers were thick and coarse compared with tornado splinters, and these weren't only wood—these were even splinters of straw and slivers of glass and metal finer than any hair. Mama groaned and shook the washcloth in her raised fist and made hissing sounds between her teeth. With every little splinter that came out of its puffed up dot of flesh, the puff collapsed. Mark looked at it with wry, twisted mouth—that must be the gas of the gas gangrene going out.

"We'll be all night," Mama suddenly moaned. "Just wash me with the cloth—I'll stand the pain. Then run and get Grandpa to come with the wagon—where is he staying all this time? Go ahead, child. Do it now! Shut your eyes, if you have to, but do it."

She dipped her washcloth in the pail and flung it to him sopping wet. "Maybe it'll slide a little better that way," she moaned.

Mark finished fast. It wasn't clean, but Mama couldn't see it. "All clean," he said.

Mama roused and opened her eyes, looked vaguely at him, as if she did not know him, or know where she was. "I think I passed out," she said fuzzily. "You're a brave boy. Now run and get the wagon!"

Mark scrambled out of the bin and ran for the door. How he loved her, she was so brave! He proudly loved her—she was braver than seven men!

7

The Looters

Mark ran all the way back across the single field and into the basement of his own barn, clutching the darkened flashlight. He had used it so long to point the hair-fine rubbish driven into Mama's legs, it had started to go dim. It mustn't be used more than a flick at a time. He still tasted the metal of the flashlight and his jaws felt strained from holding it in his mouth so long. He spat, then quickly let the flash beam angle through the dark.

Colonel was in his stall. Mr. Sayers had nailed both the other belts snug under him and at the far end of the barn Creek stood harnessed to the milk wagon. But Mr. Sayers wasn't in the barn. It puzzled Mark that under each of the wagon wheels stood a puddle of water.

Finally Mark figured he knew. The old milk

wagon had stood unused so long that its wooden wheels had shrunken and the rims around them must be loose—so loose they'd wobble off. If they did, the wheels would fall apart and the wagon would come down with Mama and hurt her still more. Satisfied that was it and that Mr. Sayers must be getting more water, Mark waited.

Colonel was sleeping on the belts. The partition groaned, it strained and creaked with the old horse's breathing. The belts had worked! They'd worked! Mark wanted to stroke Colonel's head and tell him oh, so many things . . . but Colonel was sleeping and Colonel needed sleep. So he went to Creek instead and laid his cheek against hers, loving her. Creek did not respond to him, she was still spooky from the tornado. She jerked away and the wagon backed. Mark stood there, a little forlorn. Everything was so still, and where was Mr. Sayers?

Suddenly he heard a voice. Mr. Sayers must be talking to himself. Mark grinned. But then there was a yell, an angry yell and a sound of glass smashing. Creek, scared at the sound, started backing so frantically she was going to ram the old wagon against the wall.

Mark grabbed her bridle. He steadied her

but he listened to the outside sounds. There were voices in the pasture, Mr. Sayers' voice among them. Mark snubbed Creek's lines around a post beside the wagon and snapped on the light as he ran out to the pasture.

With the beam of his light things went still. Then Mr. Sayers yelled out, "Mark, is that you? Come here fast and bring the shotgun. Load it as you come."

Mark took a moment to locate the rusty old shotgun up on a beam. He poked it down, rubbed off the cobwebs and started out of the barn on a run. Mr. Sayers had said, "Load it." Load it how? With what? He couldn't take time now to wonder.

"I'm coming," he yelled. "Where are you?"

"Over here by my roof. Hurry up, boy."

Mark came running. He thrust the gun into Mr. Sayers' hands.

"I've got four of them under the roof," he told Mark. "All right," he called out, "all of you come out with your hands up."

It was hard to see them against the black of the roof but then Mr. Sayers took the flashlight and shone it on them. But Mark looked down at a big girl lying in a sprawl right at Mr. Sayers' feet.

Mr. Sayers shook his head. "Shouldn't have

done that—didn't mean to hit her that hard.
The base of the lantern must have caught her
just right. She went down like a sack of wet
potatoes . . . but she had it coming. These four
hid under my roof when they saw my lantern,
but she came straight toward me and gave me
a big mouth. I got so mad I gave it to her with
the lantern. Of course then I was in the dark
with all five of them until you brought the gun.
Looters! That's all I need this night yet—looters."

Mr. Sayers now said in a steadier voice,
"The rims weren't going to stay on the wagon
wheels, not even after soaking with water, so I
remembered you'd said there was everything
dumped here in your pasture. Couldn't find
any more wire in the barn so I came out with
the lantern to hunt for some and these scum
saw me. They sent the girl to make sure what I
was after. Know what she said? 'How you
doing? We've got a whole pailful of stuff, besides our pockets full.' That's when I let her
have it—" The old man's voice went screechy.
"Mama in the oat bin, your dad in the hospital, people dead and dying—and they've got a
pailful!" He kicked over the pail that stood beside the girl on the ground. Watches, rings and
bracelets spilled out.

Mr. Sayers didn't even look at the jewelry. "Grab the pail," he ordered Mark, "while I hold them here with the gun. Find a puddle . . . the muddier the better, then come back and throw it over her to bring her to. *Pockets full!*"

Mark ran to the first water puddle. He wanted to hand the pail to Mr. Sayers but the old man shook his head. "No, you throw it over her. I've the gun on them."

Mark had to throw the water. The girl came up sputtering, choking and thrashing her arms. "Playing possum," the old man said scornfully. "Up with you, and in line with the others and your arms held high."

"This your daughter?" he asked the woman. "Fine way to bring up a girl."

"We didn't come out to loot," she told him. "But there it lay and we started."

Mr. Sayers did not answer her. "Go around them," he ordered Mark. "Don't get between them and the gun, keep behind them but pull everything out of their pockets—everything. We'll give them a taste of how it feels to be robbed."

"The lady and the girl too?" Mark was abashed.

"The girl most of all," Mr. Sayers snorted,

"make her feel as cheap and indecent as she is, the woman too."

Mark queasily started with the man. He pulled a billfold from the man's back pocket. "That's my own billfold," the man said.

"Good," Mr. Sayers said. "Then you know how it feels. Throw it in the pail, Mark. Now feel in his other pockets and around his waist."

It was miserable to have to feel around people and dig in their pockets.

"Can't we just throw it all on the ground ourselves?" one of the men asked. "We're not armed, we're not going to try anything in front of a gun. We'll go straight home and for what it's worth I can tell you we're going to stay there."

"All right, toss it in the pail and then the faster you disappear the less I'll be tempted to give you a spray of buckshot."

Things pinged against the metal pail as the five tossed away their loot, then they whirled and were gone in the darkness. With the shotgun to his shoulder Mr. Sayers stood watching them. Mark picked up the pail and brought it to him. Suddenly the old man broke the gun to see if there were shells inside and accidentally struck it against the pail. The sharp bang sounded loud and the dark, running figures scuttled. "Shine the flash on them," Mr. Sayers said.

"It's almost gone, it won't shine that far," Mark told him.

"They won't know. Let each of them worry about being picked out for a load of buckshot."

But the running figures were gone, there wasn't a sound and the old man dismissed them as if they had never been. He threw down the gun, picked up the pail and started for the barn. "Come on. Those five looters couldn't have picked a worse time but I guess the wagon wheels had to have time to soak and swell." He set a great pace across the pasture, but he didn't forget the wire. "See if you can find a length of wire—your eyes are young and we must save the flashlight for when we'll need it for Mama. I *would* have to smash the lantern on that girl's worthless skull."

There was wire everywhere. Mark dragged a great snaking length of it as he trotted to keep up with the old man.

In the barn he had to find his dad's tool box for Mr. Sayers. "I'm going to have to take time to clip wire and twist it around the rims—hand me a pair of pliers." Mr. Sayers wrenched with both hands at one of the wobbly wheels. "Great Jehoshaphat! This old wagon standing here all these years is ready to fall apart and oughtn't to be used at all but we've got to use it for an ambulance. It's like your Creek— they've got to be used whatever happens to them."

Mr. Sayers worked rapidly, cutting and twisting wires. He suddenly spoke up. "Looters. I don't think those five will be back, but there'll be more and my house wide open to the sky. Can you lock yours? Well, never mind, we'll nail it shut."

They didn't waste further words. They worked. Then it was done, the best it could be done. "Throw the extra wire and your dad's tool box in the wagon, Mark." Mr. Sayers didn't test anything, he just backed Creek and the wagon out of the barn. They stopped to drive three nails in the kitchen door, then they set off across the field.

Outside the blown-away barn Mr. Sayers yelled out, "Mama, we're here with a wagon."

"I'm ready," Mama called back, "I'm as ready as I ever will be."

The old man backed the wagon almost up

to the grain bin door, then he grabbed a hammer and pliers and pulled the hinges off the door.

When it was down he and Mark used the door as a ramp from the top of the grain bin to the back of the wagon. Mama, on hands and knees and in her corset and pinned-on towels, pulled herself up on it and crawled painfully to the wagon. She made dreadful sounds at every move. Then as she saw Mark's scared face she tried to laugh.

"You'd think I was a fattened pig being loaded for market. Mark, if you ever tell anyone, even your mother, about this, when I get home I'll take you over my knee and whale you."

"Oh, I wouldn't tell," Mark promised. He wanted to say something to make all this seem better. "Mama, the tornado was bad but it did bring Creek and now she can take you to the hospital."

Mama knew just how he meant it. She looked up at him. "Sure, honey, sure. But what a night like this makes a boy like you go through."

Mark nodded.

Mr. Sayers put the tailgate of the wagon up.

"Mama, the mattress is softer than oats but wouldn't you feel better if I took your corset off? You've got sheets and a blanket to cover you."

Mama looked fierce. "Old man, don't you know yet that this corset is me? It's all that holds me together. Without it I'd be just a fat, scared old woman but with it I'm still quite a gal."

"All right, Mama, but it's a long ride and it won't be over smooth roads. Can you take it? It's likely to be a long night of pain."

"What have I got here but no hope and all pain? Up on that seat, old man, and get the horse going. Mark, you hold my hand."

8

Journey into Nothing

The wobbly-wheeled milk wagon rolled
smoothly over the bare barn floor, but jolted
sharply down the squared sill no matter how
carefully Mr. Sayers eased it through the
doorway. Mama clenched her teeth but chit-
tered with pain; she flung both arms out,
grabbed the sides of the wagon. They cracked,
the old woman in her pain tore the top edges
away. The wagon was over the sill, and Mr.
Sayers stopped it right there. For all her brave
talk about what a girl she was inside her corset, it was awful what one jolt had done to
Mama, and the whole jolting journey was still
to begin.

The old man got down and came to his wife.
"Mama, you can't do that, no matter how
much it pains. Or we'd better not start at all."

His voice was husky with sympathy. "You're tearing this old dry-rot wagon apart. And what then? If the wagon goes down, you can't lie in a field on a mattress. Mark and I couldn't carry you back, and what if it rains again? And where will we go for help—everywhere everything's wrecked? That way we'd be going into nothing."

Mama lay still, letting the pain subside, but she let go of the broken sides of the wagon. "Go on," she said. "I'll pain just as much here, and let's not forget about gas gangrene. We'll go on, but give me something to grab when the jolts come. Corset!" she exclaimed. "I think I've got broken ribs under it—for the first time in my life that corset's let me down. Find something."

Mark scrambled up from beside her. He grabbed his father's heavy tool box and wedged it between the mattress and the side of the wagon. He placed Mama's hand on the handle. He looked around for something else, saw the pail of the looters and wedged it down on the other side of Mama. She clutched the rim of the pail. "That'll help," she gritted. "Something to fight and to cling to. On with it, old man."

But the barnyard was flooded and Mr. Sayers couldn't see what was under the muddy spread of puddles. The wagon bounced over a sunken pig trough, now visible as the muddy water stirred.

The heavy tool box held as Mama fought it, but she lifted the whole pail with loot and in her wrenching spilled it out over her. "What is that?" the old woman demanded, startled by the glitter and rattle.

Mr. Sayers explained as Mark scrabbled up the scattered loot.

"Looters!" Mama exclaimed. "And our house wide open to the sky."

"There ain't much left to loot—at least, nothing upstairs," the old man said bitterly. "Even the closets are sucked out and bare."

"Look," Mark yelped, scrabbling watches and rings, bracelets and lavalieres out of the bottom of the wagon. "Look, flashlights. Three of them—little ones. They threw their flashlights in the pail too."

"Give me one, and save the others so I can use each one in turn to pick out the bad spots ahead of the horse. I won't go through puddles any more, we'll have to depend on the wet grass to keep the wheels soaked and swelling.

Flashlights!" he said grimly. "So they didn't come to loot, it was just lying there and they innocently started. And I had no buckshot for them!"

"Never mind that, just drive," Mama said sharply. Then she looked startled. "Mark!" she demanded. "When you looked for a dress in my closet was there a shelf with one hatbox on it?"

"I don't know," Mark said, "I didn't look for hats."

"Hats, no! Up in my closet inside a hatbox I kept a two-gallon jar with dimes. It was almost full. I saved dimes all my life, and kept them hid in the hatbox, because men never look in hatboxes—but in it were the dimes from all my life."

"Mama," the old man said, "you're not out of your head, your mind ain't wandering? Dimes? Whatever for?"

"For this, you old fool, for a tornado and a hospital and to put a roof back on our house, and so as not to go to the poor house."

The old man sat twisted, marveling at his wife. Mark leaped from the wagon and stormed to the house.

He found the hatbox on the shelf, but

couldn't reach high enough to look into it, and he couldn't move it. "It's here, it's still here," he yelled up to the night sky out of the open closet.

In moments Mr. Sayers came up the stairs. He carried the pail with the loot still in it. "Let's pour the dimes in it too. In a pail we can carry it down together, I hope—who's to know how much two gallons of dimes weigh?"

They stumbled with the effort to get the pail of dimes back to the wagon. It took the two of them to set the pail beside Mama. Mama was crying. "No, go ahead," she wept. "With my dimes to hang on to, I can go through anything. Mark, talk to me, tell me everything that happened to you, otherwise I'll be lying here bawling."

Mark told Mama everything while the wagon zigzagged and meandered down the length of the farm with the old man sitting bent over, picking out the best paths by occasional flicks of the flashlight. Now and then Mama rocked the heavy pail in her pain, but she listened, nodded and listened to make Mark talk on. Suddenly Mark remembered the bills stuffed in his pocket and dug them out and put them in Mama's shaking hand. She clenched her fingers around them as the jolting wagon fell into the ruts of an old wagon track.

"Found the old track, we used to use to get firewood from the woodlot," the old man exclaimed. "Now if the wheels will stay together, it'll go better with them fitted in ruts."

Mama made Mark shine his flashlight. She looked at the squeezed bills. "Mark! Hundred-dollar bills—a half dozen at least!"

"Oh, there were more," Mark explained, "but I dropped them, and they went down the creek."

Mama wound the wadded bills around the tool box handle and closed her hand over them. "Dimes on the one hand, hundred-dollar bills on the other. Right now it's medicine, it's hope and everything. But somebody lost all their money and we'll turn it in—with the pail of loot—as soon as we can. The tornado let us keep our dimes, and a wagon besides—we've been lucky."

"Creek, too," Mark added eagerly. "The tornado brought Creek and Creek's bringing us to the hospital. If my dad really got Creek for me, and she didn't just come running— then I'll have Colonel, and now Creek, too."

"If he didn't, he should have, and if he didn't, I will with my dimes. If they'll sell Creek, I'll buy her for you, we've got to keep her for what she's doing for us. But, Mark, her name ought to be Hope."

Mark stoutly disagreed. "No. It's Creek, because she was in Colonel's creek, and Colonel was still alive."

"Do I have to referee a fight back there?" the old man suddenly spoke up. "What talk, you two—arguing over the name of a horse that neither one of you owns. Be quiet, I thought I heard voices." He stopped the wagon.

"Oh, the blessedness of this thing standing still," Mama whispered to Mark.

Mr. Sayers shushed her. He was sitting up straight and rigid. Creek's ears stood alert.

Mark leaned out over the side of the wagon. It wasn't voices—it seemed a single voice like over a radio or through a telephone.

"Looters?" the old man whispered. "And we ditched that gun."

Mark didn't answer. The faraway, strange mechanical voice had started again, stopped, and now there wasn't a sound in the dark fields anywhere.

"Mark, if it's looters," Mama whispered. Mark bent to her.

"If they come, sit on the pail, sit on the

dimes, and don't you stir or say anything. I'll tell them you broke your leg—old women can lie much straighter-faced than children. Sit on the dimes right now." Mama peeled the hundred-dollar bills from around the handle of the tool box and, under the sheet, stuffed them down the front of her corset. "Now let them come," she decided.

Mr. Sayers up on the seat said, "Mark, crawl over and dig in that tool box for the biggest and longest wrench you can find and hand it up to me."

"Give me one too," Mama ordered.

Mark kept the claw hammer for himself.

Each clutching his weapon, they waited, but the strange mechanical voice did not sound and no figures eased out of the woodlot back of the farm anywhere. At last the old man clucked to Creek and they moved on into the woodlot.

It was so grim and silent that Mama had to joke. "Maybe sitting warm on those dimes will hatch out more." She nudged Mark with her wrench. "But not too many, hear, I can't hold anything more down my corset."

They nervously snickered together; the old man hummed hoarse warning sounds in his throat.

The wagon moved on into the darkness under the trees, bumped over the uneven ground and exposed roots and fallen branches, for the old man did not dare use the flashlight to light his way. Nothing happened, nowhere was there a sound. Then they came to the little creek that ran shallow here with hardly any banks.

Mr. Sayers drove the wheels of the wagon into the creek. "There's no way for a wagon like this to be quiet, we're just like so many squealing pigs," he said. "I figured they've heard us anyway and are watching, waiting for us to come to them. Well, let's wait for them to come to us—at least, the creek water will do the wheels some good."

They waited and waited, and the silence under the trees closed down on them. "I'm counting up to seven thousand, five hundred and seventy-five to keep myself from screaming," Mama whispered to Mark.

As if in answer a voice close by spoke out of the waiting darkness. "All right, if you're going to play possum too, then stay right there, don't make a move, we're coming to you."

"And who are you to order me around on my own farm?" Mr. Sayers answered angrily.

"Any ordering here, I'll do. Now get off this farm, or I'll shoot." He actually raised the long-handled pipe wrench to his shoulder as if it were a gun.

Somebody laughed in the darkness. In moments they were surrounded. From everywhere dark figures stepped from behind shielding trunks of the big trees and came at the wagon.

"All right, sir, put that loaded pipe wrench down, you're scaring us to death," a laughing voice ordered.

The old man grunted disgustedly and laid the pipe wrench down on the seat in easy reach. "If you're looking for loot, there's nothing here but my badly hurt wife. I'm trying to get her to the hospital," he explained grudgingly. Then he yelled out: "Soldiers! Mama, Mark! Soldiers in uniform—not looters. Somebody at last come to help."

Mama did not answer. She was crying, and Mark let his hammer slide down the side of the pail. It was as if the whole wagon sagged with him.

"Hurt bad, hunh? That's right, we're here to help. Let's have a look. But you ain't going to get far in this chariot."

The old man chuckled dryly. "You got something better? A tornado doesn't leave you too much to pick and choose. This old milk wagon's not been used for years, but it's used tonight, and we had the horse, so we started out."

The soldier slung a walkie-talkie on his chest around to his back, shone a big flashlight up into Mr. Sayers' face, then walked around to the back of the wagon and lowered the tailgate. Mama blinked and stared into his powerful flashlight. Mark leaned down to her. "It's a walkie-talkie. That was the telephone kind of voice we heard. He's got a walkie-talkie."

Mama didn't know what a walkie-talkie was. She looked confused and blinded. The other soldiers under the trees did not come up—it must be they were covering the big man with the walkie-talkie in case anything went wrong.

The soldier took a big step from the edge of the creek into the wagon. The whole wagon tilted and tipped. The soldier jumped back. "Better drive your ark out of this water," he ordered the old man, "or if I added my weight, we'll all go over."

"Need it to keep the wheels together—the

wires aren't going to last too long once we get
on a road—if there is a clear road."

"Got more wire?" the man asked.

"Brought all kinds of it for when we'd need
more."

The big soldier—he must be the sergeant—
spoke up to his men. "Let's get more wire on
all these wheels, every few inches. Use it until
it's gone," he ordered.

Four more soldiers came up. Mark with his
foot slid the tool box along the mattress toward the sergeant. "There's all kinds of tools
in here."

The wagon ground up out of the creek. At
every wheel a man got busy winding and twisting and cutting wire. "We're proud of you,"
the big sergeant said. "At least the three of you
are trying to help yourself. Most of them can't
—so many dead and hurt, and the others act
stupefied, confused. But I guess you can't pre-
pare and set yourself for a tornado."

He stepped into the wagon, looked down at
Mama under her sheet, and grinned at the
wrench in her hand. "You may be down, but
you weren't going to take it lying down, were
you? Grandma, you're a stout girl. Okay,

sonny, you better get out of here while I have a look at your grandma."

Mark looked at Mama, he did not stir.

"Kid, that's an order," the sergeant barked. But he did not wait. He whipped the sheet off Mama. As he ripped the sheet away some of the looters' rings and things, caught in the folds, rolled over the wagon floor, glittered and gleamed in the beam of the big flashlight standing on the floor of the wagon. At once everything changed, everything became ugly.

"Now up from that pail!" the sergeant yelled. At the same time he reached across and tore Mama's wrench out of her hand. The flashlight shone on the pailful of dimes. The four men at the wheels stared.

"So the horse is bandaged and supposed to be crippled, the old woman is laid out on a mattress, but the kid sits on a pail of dimes and loot!"

"Pretty darn fancy riding horse, too, sergeant. Hardly a horse you'd hitch to a rig like this. This horse looks like quality."

"And they used to hang horse thieves from the nearest tree," the sergeant said grimly. He towered in the wagon, stood looking down on Mama and Mark. Two soldiers stood beside Mr. Sayers.

It was such a surprising sudden turn the two old people were speechless, but Mark was suddenly hotly indignant at what they'd said about Creek. "It's my horse," he yelled up at the big man. "And she is, too, hurt, she's badly cut, but we had to use her, even though my dad just gave her to me for my birthday. My dad's in the hospital and Mrs. Sayers has got to get there too. This stuff was the loot we took away from the looters that came to loot our farm— that's all it is and we're going to turn it in— with the money I found. But the dimes are Mama's from all her life. I sat on them because we thought you were looters too."

"Well, I'll be darned," the big sergeant said. "Kid, that's so crazy, I believe you."

"We held up the looters on our farm with an empty shotgun," Mark said, indignant still. "We took all the loot away, and made them put it in the pail—we even took their own billfolds away." He slapped his hand to his mouth, but it was too late. "Was that wrong? To take their own billfolds."

"Wrong? Kid, that's rich. Rich! Loot the looters. That's the only good thing I've heard all night—loot the looters."

He stood spraddle-legged in the little wagon, threw his head back and laughed. The men on the ground laughed. Then they all laughed. Mark sagged with relief.

"Put it down as our one good laugh tonight," the sergeant said as he dropped to one knee beside Mama's mattress. "Now let's look you over good." He flashed his light over the bruised, bristling legs. "Gosh, Grandma," he said, "the only thing I've seen that looks like you was a porcupine right here in a tree in your wood." He whistled. "And you took it on a bouncing wagon! I'll give you a hypo so you won't know anything the rest of the trip, won't feel a thing, and the next thing you'll know, you'll wake up in bed in the hospital. How are you under your corset and towels?" Without a word of permission he started to fumble with the corset laces.

Mama grabbed the wrench. "You unhook me, and you get this right down on your impudent head. Where were you brought up? And right before a child! You leave my corset be, I'm all right under it—I think there's broken ribs, but the corset will hold them together. And you don't stick no hypo or nothing into me!"

The big man laughed. "Okay, be modest—there were plenty tonight without even a corset left . . ." Before Mama knew what was happening, the sergeant jabbed in his hypodermic needle. "Now just lie quiet there and go to sleep."

Mama muttered, but the soldier turned to Mr. Sayers. "You know the Mason Road? It's the third one over from this farm. It's gravel, and the old road winds like a river, but it's clear all the way into town. We've got your rims wired, but take the wagon through the fields till you get to Mason Road—I doubt the wires will last otherwise. But our ambulances are using the road too, so when you get there put your wagon square across the road, flash your light, and force an ambulance to stop. Otherwise they'll go right by."

"Would there be a phone anywhere?" Mr. Sayers asked. "We ought to call the hospital —Mark's mother's there."

The sergeant shook his head. "Hail an ambulance, Dad. You go with it. Mark here can take the horse and wagon back—they won't let him in the hospital anyway. Mark, you won't be scared to come back alone?"

"I won't be scared," Mark assured him. "If I can't see my dad anyway . . . I'll wait back home for Mr. Sayers to come."

"Sergeant, what about the loot and the dimes?" one of the men spoke up from beside the wagon. "The kid alone would be fair game for looters."

"We'll bury it right here," the sergeant decided. "And mark the spot."

"No need for that," Mr. Sayers said. "I know every inch of this farm. I'll dig it up and turn the loot and money over to the police when everything is settled down."

One of the soldiers unslung a short spade strapped to his pack. They dug a hole in the soft ground beside the creek.

"What if it rains and the creek goes up again?" Mark said. "Those billfolds of the looters and all the watches will get all wet."

"Sad, isn't it?" the sergeant said. But he picked up Mark's raincoat from the wagon and they wrapped the pail in it.

"Now, Mama," the sergeant joked, "if we could strap your corset around the pail, too, nobody could get at it."

Mama did not answer. "Good," the sergeant said. "She's out like a light. Get as far as you can, Dad, before she comes to again. We'll get on, too. There's no end to this night's work, there seems almost nowhere that tornado didn't go, and it sure didn't leave any good behind."

"Thank you for everything," Mr. Sayers said. "You and your men."

"Good luck then," the sergeant said and jumped off the wagon. With his four men he melted from sight.

The wagon squealed on through the wood-lot.

9

Bareback

They were hardly started when the wagon hit a rain-bared root, the front wheels stuttered over it, but the whole body of the wagon screaked and groaned. Mr. Sayers stopped Creek before the hind wheels could bounce over the same root. He looked back, shook his head. "It isn't hurting Mama now, but a few more jolts like that and this whole thing could fall apart, and then where would we be? Mark, she doesn't need you now, come up on the seat with me, my old eyes aren't any good for this, and this silly little flashlight is no good at all."

Mark clambered up to sit beside the old man, but Mr. Sayers in the meanwhile must have had another thought. He turned the wagon around and they went back the way they'd come. "I've got to find the sergeant," the old man was muttering, "see if I can beg that big flashlight away from him."

The man wasn't hard to find. He stood alone in the field beyond the woodlot, talking orders and directions into his walkie-talkie. The four soldiers had scattered far afield.

At the sound of the wagon the man turned and shone his big flash.

"Sergeant," Mr. Sayers called out, "I bounced this wagon over a tree root, and it all but came apart. Could we have your flashlight? The little ones we've got don't pick out the holes and bumps for me. And I got to thinking . . . Wouldn't it be something if we made it to Mason Road and they wouldn't see our little toy flashlights, and we'd get run down by an ambulance?"

The sergeant laughed. "Shrewd thinking to get my flashlight away from me." He came over to the wagon.

"It's really Mark I'm thinking of. He's got to come back alone to an empty house."

"I'm not scared," Mark protested. "Not with Creek—and not when we're going back to Colonel. If I'm scared in the house, I'll stay in the barn with them."

"Good boy!" the sergeant said. "Just don't

take them into the *living* room with you."
Laughing, he handed up his flashlight and took
Mr. Sayers' tiny one. "No good to me either
but I'll take it until I find another one. You
can find about anything on a night like this,
even a pailful of dimes."

"Don't go making fun of Mama's dimes.
They're going to put the roof back on our
house, maybe buy us a bed—if they don't,
we'll sleep in the oats in the grain bin."

"Don't worry, you'll get help," the sergeant
assured him. "The Red Cross is already in
Stanton. Things will soon straighten out. Now
on your way lest Mama comes to before you
get to the Mason Road. She's quite a girl, that
wife of yours. She didn't whimper but she must
have gone through holy hell until I gave her
that shot. Almost tempted to give her a booster
but I'd better not, I'm not hep enough on that
kind of stuff, so make it fast to an ambulance."

"Sergeant," Mark spoke up, "could you give
Creek a hypo in her leg? She's limping bad."

The big man shook his head. "All I could do
would be to put her to sleep so she'd lie down.
You ask the men on the ambulance, they're
interns. They may have something to ease the
pain. They'll do it for you if they can. I'll give

out the word on my walkie-talkie my first contact."

"But suppose Creek gets crippled forever?"

The big man smiled at him. "And suppose Mama doesn't get to the hospital, suppose Mr. Sayers doesn't find out about your dad, suppose he doesn't get to see your mother, 'suppose' . . ."

Mark grinned sheepishly. "All right, I get it. Giddap, Creek."

The old man handed him the flashlight. "You shine the way and pick out the best way across the field. When I get back we'll spend the rest of the night doctoring Creek. I'm an old horseman, raised horses all my life, doctored 'em too—that's what the oats in the grain bin were from."

Oats! Mother had been going to bring some for Colonel, but instead the tornado had come. Now there were oats in the bin. They'd make Colonel strong and maybe help heal Creek's cut.

They zigzagged through the fields, now they'd soon come to the Mason Road. Mama was still sleeping and the milk wagon moved smoothly through the grass. The tornado hadn't touched down here at all. Then the flash beam picked a gray line far out ahead. "The Mason Road," Mark yelled.

"About time," the old man said.

And then they were in the gravel road. Creek rested and Mark jumped down to look at her bandaged leg. Mr. Sayers came down stiffly from the wagon and studied it, too. The bandage was still in place but above it the flesh was puffed out and swollen. "That's from the tight bandage—but it's got to be. The moment I get to your house we'll loosen the bandage, but while you're there alone don't you touch it no matter how badly it swells. If she's hurting, she'd kick like a mule. Understand?"

Mark nodded. He hated Creek to be hurting.

They stood and stood and nothing moved along the road. Nothing came. "The sergeant said it might be a long wait—we're not the only ones," Mr. Sayers cautioned Mark. But finally he became impatient himself. Suddenly he could stand no more. "What if no ambulance comes for hours, and Mama comes to, and then still we have to go all the miles into the hospital? You get in the back with the light. Keep shining it from wheel to wheel and watch the wires. We'll stop before the last one wears through, but we'll at least be doing something instead of standing here. The sergeant said this road was clear so I won't need any light ahead. You keep it on the wheels and watch like a hawk."

"But what'll I do going back without any wires on the wheels?"

"Have you ever ridden a real riding horse bareback?"

Mark gave him a startled look. "Yes, yes I have. I never told anyone, but on the way to school there's a house with a yard for their riding horse. I used to feed him sugar. Once I climbed the fence and got on his back. He threw me. I fell under him and he stepped right over me and he came back and nuzzled me until I remembered and reached a cube of sugar up to him. Then he let me get on again and we rode and rode. I was late to school but it was worth it."

"Threw you and you got on again! You'll be all right with horses! Look, if you ride Creek back, it'll be a lot easier on her than dragging the wagon. This wagon isn't important, we'll leave it at the side of the road when the ambulance comes."

"What'll we do with Dad's tool box?"

"We'll hide it back of bushes in a ditch. Now hop in and watch the rims."

As Mr. Sayers said the words there was a roar and an ambulance came hurtling out of the night and they hadn't put the wagon across the road to block it. Mark waved the flashlight but the ambulance shot by. Mr. Sayers groaned and said, "Kick me for being such a wise guy and knowing better than the sergeant."

They went on down the road at a slow careful pace because of Creek's bad limp. Mark stood in the box of the wagon shining the flash from wheel to wheel and then on Creek's awful limp. It scared him but it scared him to look at Mama lying there so dead-looking. He knew they had to get to the hospital.

The steel-rimmed wheels dug into the gravel. Then came the first sharp ping as the tightly wound wire snapped and sprang away. After the first one they all seemed to go. At last Mark said, "We'll have to stop."

The old man looked around. One of the rims was riding off the wheel. He stopped Creek. There was no sound anywhere, nothing moved. The few stars of the evening had gone away. The old man clucked to Creek and turned the wagon crosswise in the road. They waited.

It seemed hours before there was a roaring far down the road. "Now wave the flashlight in circles and up and down. It's got to see us long before it gets here if it's going to stop in time. Be ready to jump if I have to drive down in the ditch."

Then there was time for nothing. The ambulance roared down on them, squealed to a stop and slewed in the gravel. It was scary for a moment, then two men jumped down.

They had the tailgate down by the time Mr. Sayers struggled down from the seat.

"Good," one of the men said, "she's on a mattress. We'll take mattress and all, because all the room left is on the floor."

"Your wife?" the other man asked. "Then you sit on the floor with her and hold her steady. Do the best you can. We've got a man in there hurt bad—whole church caved down on him. What about this kid?"

"He's going back. Mark, once you get to a level spot unhitch the wagon and let it stand. Keep Creek's harness on—if her leg gives out and she goes down, you'll have something to hang on to. . . . My wife's had a hypo a while back, the sergeant thought maybe she'd need a booster."

The intern shook his head. "No, better wait. Don't want to interfere with what the docs might give her. We'll be in the hospital in a few minutes."

"Please, mister," Mark said. "Could you give Creek the hypo you're not going to give Mama? It's a long way back home and she's limping bad."

"Creek? Oh, the horse."

"Could you?" Mr. Sayers said urgently. "Mark's never ridden her and if she went wild with pain . . . wouldn't it slow her down?"

The man shrugged. "I'm no horse doctor, still it probably would make her more manageable."

Mark held Creek's head while the man jabbed the needle into her leg. He jabbed it in a circle around the puffing. "Ought to make her more comfortable. Lots of luck, son. This is the kind of crazy thing you do on a night like this—horse doctor!"

He jumped back in the ambulance. Mr. Sayers was already inside by Mama. The ambulance roared away. It was gone and Mark was alone with Creek.

He walked her on the grassy edge of the road. When they came to a brush pile he stopped, pulled the tool box out and hid it back of the bushes. Then he led Creek away from the brush pile so the abandoned wagon wouldn't give the tool box away. But he didn't go far. Creek's slow weary limp worried him. He unhitched her and put the flashlight on the wagon seat so he could reach out for it after he had mounted.

They went along the grassy side of the road until at last there were the wagon tracks leading out of the field. Now he wouldn't get lost. He could find his way back by the crushed tracks the wagon wheels had made in the grass.

It was so still, so alone. But he had a flashlight and there would be Colonel when they got home and all three of them would stay together in the barn until Mr. Sayers came. It was better to think about that than to think about who might be in the silent fields. Now only one more road to cross, then through the Sayers' farm and across the single field and then Colonel would neigh a welcome from the barn because he would hear Creek.

It seemed that this whole night—everything

they'd gone through together—had made Creek his. Why, he'd told the sergeant that his dad had given her to him for his birthday and the big man hadn't questioned it. It had to be so.

Oh, what if in the hospital the first thing Dad said to Mother was: "Did you find that horse I got for Mark? I left her in the wood-lot."

And then faintly across the dark fields there was the walkie-talkie voice. He listened closely but he must have imagined it. There was nothing but silence.

Suddenly Mark was uneasy. Suppose the big sergeant was at some farm down the road and a man there was saying, "I lost my horse. She ran away in the tornado. She's a brown riding horse, have you seen her?"

And the sergeant would say, "A brown horse, with a star on her forehead?"

"That's her," the man would say.

"Funny, we saw a horse like that pulling a crazy, little wagon. Didn't seem to go together —horse was too fine. But the boy said he'd just got her for his birthday. Well, if she's your horse, she won't be hard to find. It's a farm on the Stanton road. The man said it hadn't been touched by the tornado—it'll be one of the few that wasn't. Give it a try. It might be your horse."

Mark shuddered and was glad he'd left the wagon on the road. He stared ahead. Maybe the man was out looking for Creek right now.

He'd made it all up from imagining the walkie-talkie, but now it was as real as the night. He wouldn't take Creek home to the barn. He'd go to the woodlot—that's what he'd do. He'd lead Creek down in the gully to the same crotch that had held Colonel. Nobody'd see her down there in the dark—she was dark, too. But he'd stay with her. He'd stay until Mr. Sayers came. Mr. Sayers wouldn't let anybody take Creek away from him. Maybe by that time he'd find out from Dad that Dad had bought her.

Mark lay over Creek and whispered in her ear. Together they went quietly through the deep dark to their own woodlot trees on their own farm.

10

Down in the Gully

They came into their own woodlot and it was dreamlike silent under the stately trees, with only the little creek susurrusing its tiny baby talk. Mark walked Creek into the water to let her drink before marching her up the gully and prisoning her in the crotch of the fallen tree. He was pleased at her slow, dreamy amble without any limp at all. The good doctor in the ambulance must have really cured Creek with the shots he had put around her leg—a ring block he had called it. The leg was still miserably puffed out, but Mr. Sayers had said not to touch the bandage, not to loosen it.

It must be way after midnight. Why, then it was his birthday right now! It was the morning of his very own birthday, but here it felt as if it were Creek's and Colonel's birthday, too—all of them together, everything had worked out so well for them all.

At the beginning of the deep gully, Mark halted Creek and slid down. He took down the rolled-up driving lines and led her over the tornado-roughed-up ground into the tangle of upside-down trees. Nothing was scary now, just tired and sleepy and dreamy. Mark yawned a stretching great yawn. Creek jerked up her head and stared wide-eyed at him. He led her on carefully around every tangle and they slow-stepped over tree trunks.

Now Creek was suddenly dreamy no more. She acted alarmed, her hide began to shiver as it had done when he'd first found her in the creek. Mark talked to her softly as he eased her into the crotch of the great tree—the crotch narrowed down to nothing and would keep her, as it had Colonel, from putting her weight down on her hurt leg.

Mark had to pull branches aside that had sprung back into place after Colonel had walked them down in backing out. Now there was only the thickest branch left, the one that, if he pushed it back in place behind Creek across the V of the crotch, would lock her in as if she were in a stall.

The branch was springy and tough, and

slippery from its wet, pasted leaves. It was so stout Mark could hardly keep both hands gripped around it, suddenly it sprang out of his grasp like coiled steel, slashed like a bullwhip across Creek's leg, across the bandage, across the cut. Creek gave a scream that tore through the gully and split the silence of the night. She screamed again and reared straight up in her scare, her forefeet pawed at the crotch, then her hind legs slipped from under her in the wet muck and she went down, all four legs madly kicking out against the small branches of the crotch. Then she slid down and lay on her side under the tree, but still she thrashed on. The hurt leg got caught in the tangle of branches and her too wild, too loose harness. The bandage came loose, unrolled and unfurled.

Mark crawled under the thick branch of the crotch to get to her head, to hold her and talk her out of thrashing, she mustn't hurt herself still more. For a moment Creek lay still, wild eyes watching him, but as Mark came close she flung her head away from him. She was afraid of him! She showed her teeth and screamed at him. Mark, feeling sick and gaggy in his horror, crawled away so as not to make her kick out more with the cut leg, caught and doubled-up in the harness.

It was him Creek was scared of. Creek thought he had hit her with the branch. Mark started to crawl back as if to tell her it had been an accident. Creek wouldn't allow it, she began thrashing, she kicked the leaves down on the ground into a horrible storm. He couldn't do anything for her—she hated him, she thought he had done it on purpose.

Mark forced himself away and, beyond the fallen tree, clambered up the steep gully bank. He kept slipping because he kept looking back at Creek. She was quieting now that he was gone from her sight, she wasn't kicking any-more. Mark briefly shone the flashlight on her, then noiselessly climbed the gully bank.

On top of the bank he sat down in the mucky wetness and did not care how awful it felt, because he felt awful. Creek thought he had done it on purpose and now she was scared of him. He *had* done it, even if it was by accident. He didn't dare flash the light down in the gully now. He didn't know what to do—maybe if she knew he was sitting here, even that would be bad for her.

At last there seemed nothing to do but to go away. Maybe if he went away, Creek could somehow get up—the branch had hit her, she wasn't locked into the crotch by it now. Maybe she'd want to come to the barn to Colonel. In darkness, without light to help him, he forced himself to go away from Creek.

At last in the barn Mark snapped on the flashlight. Colonel was awake and up on his feet. The old horse whipped his head sharply around and neighed a great welcome out at Mark. Maybe Creek would hear and want to come. At least Colonel still liked him—of course, Colonel didn't know what he'd done to Creek. Mark tried to tell Colonel friendly fond things, but his voice wouldn't come out of his throat.

Colonel nosed around in his empty crib and looked back at Mark again. Colonel needed something to eat. It lifted Mark's spirits. After what he had done to Creek, he needed to do something good for Colonel. He thought of the potatoes in the cellar, but the kitchen door was nailed shut, and the tornado had driven the trap door so tight into its frame he doubted he could tug it out again. Mark dreaded going by way of the musty cellar up into the empty house where no one was and no one would come. Maybe even Mr. Sayers wouldn't be able to come all this night.

Mark thought of his play-pile of hay in the loft of the barn. It was old hay, short and stubbly and dry and dusty, but it would be better than nothing. Maybe Colonel could munch on it some.

Up in the hay barn Mark stood amazed as he flashed his light all around the barn floor. The tornado in passing by the barn doors had sucked all the hay and dust, even the cobwebs, out of the barn. The floor lay sucked out and clean as if it had been vacuumed. He could shine the flashlight through the cracks in the floor and see Colonel down in his stall. The play-pile hay must have gone in the tornado too. He felt too tired and forlorn to climb the ladder. Huh, Mother had promised him oats and tonic for his birthday! It was his birthday!

A thought leaped at him. In the kitchen was a whole bottle of vitamins. Wouldn't a whole bottle—no, half of it—help Colonel just like a tonic? He'd give Colonel half and keep the other half for Creek—in case she came. It would mean he'd have to go down through the cellar, the claw hammer was in the tool box in the ditch, so he couldn't open the nailed kitchen door. But half of a bottle for Colonel! And the half-bottle waiting for Creek would make it seem as if Creek must come.

Mark found a spade, then, with the big flashlight shining, he marched himself resolutely to the cellar trap door. It took a lot of prying and straining with the flat spade but finally he forced the door up out of its frame. He looked down into the yawning dark cellarway. Then he grabbed up the flashlight and rushed headlong down the steps and on up the stairway to the dining room. In the kitchen he snatched the bottle of vitamins and flew back over the rolling potatoes and out of the quiet place.

Once out, he flashed the light back of him down the cellarway and saw the potatoes. He shuddered. No, he couldn't sit down there and cut potatoes for the horses. But he had oats— why, he did have oats!

"Oats! Oats!" he said happily. There were oats in the Sayers' grain bin! He'd screen and sift the dust and dirt out of them. Mark dashed up the slant of the open trap door and yanked the half-screen down from the storeroom window. With the screen and the flashlight he galloped across the single field to sift oats in the Sayers' wide-open barn.

It seemed to have taken tired hours and hours to sift the oats, but now Mark was back in his own barn. Creek had not come, there was no Creek with Colonel, and nothing moved anywhere in the pasture.

Mark showed Colonel his spilling-full pail of oats, but did not give any to him. He first rubbed the half-bottle of vitamin capsules into Colonel's mouth, then spilled half of the pail of oats into Colonel's crib. Mark kept the biggest half for Creek and planted the half-bottle of vitamins in the oats as if it were a candle, waiting for Creek. Colonel munched on oats, and it was a comforting, homey sound, except that Mark felt too tired to appreciate anything. Oh, he was tired, his jaws kept cracking out big wrenching yawns, then almost wouldn't go back in their sockets again. It hurt, and he was so tired.

Still there was one more thing he ought to do—he ought to go back to the gully, maybe now after all this time Creek wouldn't be scared of him anymore. But what if she struggled again when she saw him, and hurt herself worse, hurt herself so she'd be a cripple forever?

Mark did not dare take the chance. But one thing he could do if Creek should free herself and still come to the barn. There was no room for her in Colonel's stall—not with the thresh-ing machine belts holding Colonel up—but Creek would want to be close to the old horse. The upper barn was all sucked out, what if there should be something left of the packed-down hay pile in the haymow? The hay would make a fine bed for Creek to lie down in right close next to Colonel's stall.

With a long sigh, followed by an endless yawn, Mark searched out a pitchfork and wearily climbed with it to the haymow. Amaz-ingly his play pile still was in its corner—the only thing left in the upper barn by the passing tornado.

The night's stillness stood as heavy as its darkness, but he seemed too tired to turn the flashlight on. With the pitchfork stuck in the hay, Mark leaned on it so heavily, his hands slid down the smooth, worn handle almost to the tines, and he almost went down on his face. He was too tired to move hay and Mr. Sayers would never come, and Mother had to stay with Dad in the hospital. There was no-body to come and help him, and he couldn't help Creek because she was afraid of him— Creek hated him.

Still leaning hard on the dug-in pitchfork,

Mark found himself staring into the opening of the little tunnel he had made—it seemed years ago, but it had been just before the tornado. Oh, but the little tunnel looked safe and good. Safe to sleep and hide in. He'd take the flashlight with him for company and sleep under the hay. If he set the lit flashlight shining on him, his body would block out the light from the mouth of the tunnel so nobody coming to search for Creek would find him. He needed light, even if he fell asleep with it shining full in his face. It was so lonely here, he felt so awful about Creek that it made everything awful, it was worse than being scared of the dark.

He wouldn't sleep really anyway. Mr. Sayers when he came would call his name, and he'd hear, and together they'd go down to Creek.

Mark sighed at the thought as he lay stretched in his tunnel, cradled his head in his arms, and fell asleep with his cheek pillowed on the hard casing of the rectangular flashlight.

Down in the basement Colonel munched oats with tired, slow, worn old teeth.

11

Cookie Breakfast

Mark woke in his stuffy, hot tunnel under the hay pile and lifted his numb cheek off the flashlight. He looked at the sharp daylight standing at the mouth of the tunnel. The sun was shining! Mr. Sayers hadn't come and it was day.

Shaking the warm sleep feeling out of his head Mark climbed down the hayloft ladder to the basement of the barn. Creek wasn't there. Only Colonel neighed out at him and then went on munching oats. Colonel was still eating. He'd take the half-pail of oats and the half-bottle of vitamins out to Creek and maybe in the sunlight she wouldn't be afraid of him. He'd bring water to her from the creek.

The pail stood empty beside Colonel's stall and the vitamins were gone. Somebody had been in the barn while he slept and had fed Colonel the rest of the oats. It must have been Mr. Sayers, but where had he gone? Creek must still be in the gully—maybe dead, maybe bleeding to death with her cut kicked open, and here he'd slept right through the whole night!

He'd run to the gully with the pail and a knife and the mattress cover. He'd make bandages and bandage her leg, then he'd lead her up to the barn to be with Colonel and then he'd go back to the grain bin and get oats for her.

Mark looked around for the mattress cover —it was gone, and they'd only cut one strip from it for a bandage. Had Mr. Sayers found Creek and gone to bandage her?

Mark's thoughts raced but they raced in circles. . . . He was so hungry! He hadn't had any supper, the tornado had come before supper, and afterward. . . . Now he knew—he'd quick run to the house and get the cookie jar. No, he ought to run to the grain bin to see if Mr. Sayers was there. No, he couldn't run, he was too hungry to run there, his stomach leaped in a ravenous greed at the thought of cookies— handfuls! He raced toward the house but he felt shamed—guilty to have hunger while maybe Creek lay in the gully.

The kitchen door was still nailed shut but the trap door was open. He tore up the cellar steps and snatched the cookie jar from its shelf in the kitchen, popped it in the pail and started for the cellar stairs. He wouldn't eat a single cookie until he got to Creek.

Heck, he could eat as he ran. He unscrewed the top of the jar and then out of the stillness came a harsh rasping sound that filled the house. Mark dropped the handful of cookies and stood rigid as his hair rose like hackles on the back of his neck. Then the sound came again and he giggled sheepishly. It was a snore! He ran through the kitchen into the dining room and around to the living room, the cookie jar banging in the tin pail.

On the sofa lay Mr. Sayers in all his clothes —even his shoes. He'd spread the mattress cover under him to keep the sofa clean. "What?" He sat up. "What is it? I'm coming, Mama."

Then he sat and stared. "Mark!" he finally said. "Boy, where were you, where've you been? I searched all over both our farms half the night. Where were you?"

"Under the hay pile in my tunnel," Mark said guiltily. Then it burst out. "I fell asleep, I was only going to sleep a little while until I could go back to Creek or if you came we could both go. . . . I never heard you—and Creek is still in the gully and she's probably dead, she's kicked herself to pieces. The bandage came off and she hates me and she wouldn't let me help her and I did it all because I tried to hide her from the man that was coming to claim her. . . . I couldn't stand it and I went to sleep, I did it and all I could do was lie there and sleep!" Mark was crying and choking out words at the same time.

"You talk more than Mama does when she first wakes up," Mr. Sayers said grumpily. "Now tell it over. Tell it slowly and in order, but don't you stand there crying because you fell asleep. I fell asleep too. There comes a time when your wornout carcass calls a halt. Then you sleep as if someone'd hit you with an ax. Now blow your nose and stop that crying. Even if Creek's dead—and I doubt it—she saved Mama's life last night. All right, now we'll go and see to her but only if you give me a handful of those cookies." Mr. Sayers made a face. "Cookies! In all my seventy-some years

I've never had a breakfast of cookies—what a tornado doesn't do to you! I didn't have any supper—guess you didn't either, so we'll chew on cookies instead of getting breakfast right now. Don't worry, we'll save a few for Creek, she must be hungry too."

Mr. Sayers seemed sure that Creek would be alive. They walked out through the cellar-way. Then Mr. Sayers stopped. "Don't you want to know about your dad?"

Mark set down the pail and stared aghast. He hadn't even thought about his dad or his mother—just about Creek. He hadn't thought once!

Mr. Sayers grinned. "Don't look so spanked, boy. We've been through too much. . . . They can't say much about your dad yet. It's a concussion. He's out like a light but the doctors think he'll be all right. Your mother's going to stay with him and Mama. There just aren't enough nurses, so many people hurt in the tornado. But she says to tell you she'll come flying home the moment she can get away. And Mama, besides bristling like a por-cupine with rubbish, had three broken ribs under that corset and a broken leg. Think of it, she crawled into the wagon like that! Stout girls our women—your mother only cried when I told her you hadn't even a scratch, just a couple more freckles. Now I ask you, are freckles something to cry about?"

Mark had a few tears himself but to hide them he hugged the old man.

"Okay," Mr. Sayers said, "now we'll go to Creek. But first another handful of those gooey cookies, and on the strength of them we'll carry that horse of yours home if we have to."

Mr. Sayers talked all the length of the pasture. There wasn't time to think for all the listening Mark had to do. "I got a ride back in an empty ambulance as far as where you left the wagon," Mr. Sayers said. "And I followed your tracks down to the middle of my woodlot— there I lost them. And when I got here you were nowhere. I yelled like crazy and I went all over both our farms. And then it was morning so I fed Colonel and fell down on the couch in your living room like a poled ox."

"I slept like a poled ox in my tunnel," Mark said. "What's a poled ox?"

"That's you and me, and now we're full of cookies," Mr. Sayers joked. "I've got your bottle of vitamins in my pocket and my leg is sore from sleeping on them. I suppose they're for Creek."

They were going to Creek and Mr. Sayers was telling him everything about the hospital. Mark stumbled on beside him too absorbed to watch where he was going. Mr. Sayers talked to him just as if he were a grown-up. Now that he didn't have his wife to talk to he talked to him, Mark, as if he were as big as Mama. He gave a little choked-off giggle.

"Now what are you snickering about?" Mr. Sayers asked.

Mark had to tell, but it *was* funny, he didn't mind, he hardly hesitated. "I was imagining myself as fat and as big as Mama."

"Oh, so?" Mr. Sayers wasn't a bit angry. "Well, you can just stop imagining it. What if it worked? Then I'd have to lift you over fences, but you'd be so heavy that I couldn't and we'd both go down in one fat heap and there we'd lie and both begin to sprout from all this rain."

Oh, Mr. Sayers was wonderful. Now he'd suddenly found a friend—a wonderful talking friend. Wasn't it strange that before the tornado Mr. Sayers had just talked to Dad or to Mother except that now and then he'd toss a joke to him like you tossed a cookie to a little dog.

"Mr. Sayers, I like you!" Mark burst out.

"Well, if that's so, then don't keep calling me 'Mr. Sayers' so polite, as if I were a stranger. Call me Grandpa."

Mark tried it: "I like you, Grandpa."

"I like you, too, because, you know, I never had a son. Just girls—four girls, not one single little runty, skinny boy. I tell you, a man can hardly stand it. I couldn't have stood it at all if I hadn't loved them so."

Mark jumped up and down at his sudden thought. "It's too late for me to be your son, isn't it? But, Grandpa, I could be your grandson, couldn't I? Even late?"

"It's a deal," Grandpa answered promptly. "Late, but high time, I'd say, because my four girls have only girl babies themselves. But right now you've cured all that—Grandson!"

They shook hands on it, standing solemnly before each other in the middle of the pasture.

Grandpa walked on to get Creek but Mark stood there. You got to a spot—like now in the middle of a field—and on that spot you became a grandson, and on your birthday. Mark let his grandpa walk on, but he stayed long enough to thrust a stick into the soggy ground in the exact spot where he'd become Grandpa's grandson. Then he galloped after his grandfather. Later he'd put up a better marker but now he couldn't bear to be separated from his new grandpa. Now he was Mark, with a grandpa and two horses.

They went into the gully by way of the woodlot, because Grandpa was old like Colonel and couldn't get down the steep side of the gully, except maybe in a tornado. But as they neared the tree of the big crotch and saw Creek lying there motionless, Mark dropped behind. When Grandpa waited for him Mark explained, "I'd better stay here, Creek thinks I did it and she hates me. She might start kicking again if she saw me."

"I doubt it," Grandpa said. "I doubt that very much. You just come right along with me and bring that jar of cookies and then we'll see who hates who. She won't get alarmed. See, in her struggles she worked her collar up over her head and the padding under the collar slipped down over her eyes. You know what? I think that saved her from any more struggling. And you know something else? I don't think it was you that scared her into panic when that branch slashed across her leg. I think it was the upside-down trees with those white roots sticking up. I think when she got caught in the tornado she must have seen trees go up and come down like that. And now roots sticking up like that spook her. We'll see. We'll leave the padding over her eyes and you feed cookies to her while I work her out of that tangle of harness."

Breathing his hope, Mark squatted noiselessly down before Creek's head and pushed a cookie between her lips that had begun trembling. But Grandpa talked soothing things to her while he pulled away branches and stripped away the harness, but all the time he kept away from her hoofs.

Creek ate cookies and lay still. Then Grandpa said, "Now I think you'd better run to the creek and get her a pailful of water. It isn't easy for her to swallow lying down and with a throat as long as hers the poor girl must be cookie crumbs all the way down. First give me your shirt—that ought to be just about the right length to tie over her eyes. The collar pad will fall off as soon as I strip off the harness."

Mark took off his shirt. Grandpa looked at him and saw him shaking, but he said nothing about it, instead he took the shirt and studied it. "What a dirty shirt—where you been—in a tornado?"

Grandpa seemed to know just when to say a goofy thing. It kept you from going all heavy and scared down in your stomach.

When Mark returned with the sloshing pail Grandpa had Creek up on her feet so she could drink properly. She sucked the whole pail empty and she wasn't scared of him at all, but, of course, Grandpa had tied the shirt over her eyes. "Just 'till we get her away from this mess of roots. Then you'll see, I'll let you pull the shirt off her eyes and you'll find out it was the trees and not anything you did. How could Creek hate you?"

Mark marveled at all Grandpa knew about horses. "How is her cut?" he asked.

Grandpa shrugged. "Worse, of course. Gone deeper, but that was from pulling the wagon because the wound didn't bleed at all here, not after she kicked the bandage off. So you didn't even harm her that way. In fact it was good, with the bandage gone her leg isn't puffed up anymore. There's only one thing—flies. I didn't want to but I had to put the bandage back on so the flies couldn't get into the wound. Just so they haven't already laid their eggs. I'd hate to have to pour anything strong enough to prevent maggots into that raw gash. She'd kick like a steer and rip the gash even deeper."

Mark was rigid with horror. Sour water washed around his teeth. He gagged at the thought of maggots. "But you said the bandage shouldn't be tight."

"We'll see. It'll be hard to keep flies out of the wound except with tight bandages, but I really think that exercise—just walking around in the air and sun—would heal her better than anything. But how to keep the danged flies out?"

"Feed sacks," Mark yelled. "There's a stack of them in the barn. Couldn't we put her leg in a sack and tie it shut on top? It'd be like a stocking."

"Mark," Grandpa said, "when they put you in the world they didn't forget to screw your head on, did they?"

Grandpa led Creek out of the woodlot and Mark walked proudly behind.

Then they were in the lane that led to the barn, and Grandpa stopped Creek. He handed Mark the bridle. "Now you lead her. I'll walk behind. Pull that shirt away from her eyes, and you'll see it was the trees that panicked her—not anything you did. Then you march fast so I can cook us some breakfast—bacon and eggs, and eggs and bacon, and some coffee and a little bacon for dessert—but not one gooey cookie."

Mark hardly listened as he pulled the shirt

from Creek's eyes. She blinked and stared, then threw back her head and neighed out over the field. From the barn Colonel neighed an echo. And then Creek reached down and nuzzled Mark's hair with soft, nibbling lips. Mark walked with his face straight forward on account of Grandpa behind and because he didn't want Grandpa to see him cry. Oh, it was wonderful.

"Now bacon and eggs," Grandpa said. "Now you'll enjoy them."

"Can you cook too?" Mark marveled.

"As a cook, Mark, I can tell you, I should be lined up against a wall and shot with burned bacon," Grandpa said. "But seeing for the next few days I've got to keep us alive, I'll only cook if you promise not to shoot me for my cooking. We'll fix Creek up with a feed sack and throw some hay down for a soft bed for her, then you and I will begin batching it with bacon and eggs and the first one that can't swallow them is an old maid."

Mark couldn't answer. Creek was hobbling and crippling almost like a dog on three legs but she was going to the barn—his barn—and Colonel was there to comfort her.

12

Farmer Breakfast with Coffee

They both wiped their mouths with the backs of their hands—Mark did it right after Grandpa. Then he did it again with the back of his other hand. They'd had breakfast and they'd finished every last crumb. It had been enormous. Bacon and eggs and fried potatoes —a farmer's breakfast, enough for a man. Then still coffee—he'd even had coffee, black without cream, just like Grandpa's. Well, his had had some sugar in it, but he hadn't stirred up the sugar.

"Now do I have to find the shotgun and shoot you with burnt bacon up against the barn wall?" Mark asked. He rubbed his stomach and purred with contentment to show Grandpa it was all a big joke.

Grandpa grinned. "Nope, don't think I deserve that. Cooked everything just fine, even surprised myself."

Mark wiped the back of his hand over his mouth again. Grandpa hadn't even thought of napkins—hadn't thought of orange juice or milk, but had given him coffee instead. Mother would have been speechless. But no fruit juice, no milk, no napkins, and nobody fussing about any of them—he sure wasn't reminding Grandpa of any of those woman-fussy things!

Grandpa seemed to purr with contentment, too, and gave himself a second cup of coffee. "Ah," he said, "good solid food and coffee to float it down sure beats your cookies. But that's what a man needs after missing his supper. We sure were hollowed-out men, and we've got work to do. But that's good, work cures about everything except a sore back—it takes away worries and helps waiting. And that's what we're going to have to do—wait. By now they must have started to clear the highway between Stanton and town, and then the buses will ride again. And linemen are no doubt swarming all over the telephone poles and the light wires, then in a day or two you can talk to your mother by telephone. Meanwhile it's best you and I clear the pasture, so that tractors can get at my roof and cranes can lift it back on the house walls again. Then when Mama is better and can be moved, she'll have a roof over her head and a bedroom. Hey, we'd better remember to hammer a bed together from all those parts scattered all over your pasture."

"What's a concussion?" Mark abruptly demanded.

"Thinking about your dad? Well, that's the idea of all this pasture-clearing work—it's to keep us from thinking and worrying, and to help us wait. A concussion! Remember how you and I fell asleep last night, me here, you under the hay pile? I said then it was as if we'd been hit with an ax. Well, it's something like that with a concussion. It knocks you out, you go to sleep and lie there sleeping for days. But when you come to, you're usually in pretty good shape again."

"But then Dad can't tell Mother whether he got Creek for my birthday, and then I won't know, and what if somebody comes and claims her and takes her away? And how will Dad eat? And if he doesn't eat, won't he be too weak to talk?"

"How that mind of yours works! Now what do I answer from all that ruck of questions? Don't worry, your dad will sleep and they'll feed him right while he sleeps—right through his veins."

Mark sighed his relief. A big hospital sure was wondrous and puzzling and strange. "But couldn't Mother come home, if Dad just sleeps? Does she need to watch him sleep?"

Grandpa hesitated. "Remember, there's Mama too, for your mother to watch. And it —it's a different kind of sleep, more like being unconscious, only a little bit different from that too. But meanwhile they'll not only be feeding him, they'll be giving him medicine through his veins too, and all the time he lies there without wasting his strength talking, he'll heal like mad."

"Then shouldn't I go to Mother, if Mother can't leave Dad?"

"Of course you should, and of course you will as soon as the highway is cleared and the buses run. But it's too far to walk, it'd take us all day, and Creek here needing tending to, and Colonel too. But I've got it all figured out. Your mother needs to see you and you need to see her, so we'll give her a free hour away from that hospital room. I think I might be able to persuade her to go out with you for an hour or two, while I watch instead. Then you two can sit over an ice cream soda, or two, or three, and talk yourselves out. I've got an idea if we don't do that soon, your mother will go into such little pieces from wanting to see you, even a carpenter like your dad wouldn't be able to hammer her together again."

Mark sat wriggling with delight. Then he jumped up. "Let's go to work—let's clear the whole pasture."

"Well, maybe," Grandpa said. "But first let's just clear a path to my roof for the tractors, it isn't going to go as fast as all that."

"There's an old stoneboat lying in the grass up against the end of the barn," Mark told him excitedly. "If we could hitch Colonel and Creek to that, we could clear the pasture just like nothing."

"With Creek's cut leg?"

"Oh, no," Mark said regretfully. "But you said exercise would heal the cut faster," he argued.

"Exercise, but not strain. We'll just use Colonel, and Creek can hobble along but not work. Work would be good for Colonel though. It ought to limber up his stiff old legs even better than this liniment I brought."

Mark jumped at the word. Unable to wait, he raced away to the barn. They let the belt straps down from under Colonel and backed him out of the stall.

They rubbed all Colonel's four legs with the liniment. It stained his white hide brown, and it stung and smarted in Mark's eyes and throat, but he rubbed on and on. "Oh, this is strong! It ought to make Colonel's legs all strong and better. Shall we use it on Creek too?"

"No, hardly," the old man said. "At least, not on her sore leg. And I doubt how strong it's going to make Colonel but at least he smells good and strong." He coughed and had to hurry to the doorway to get some air and blow his nose. Mask still rubbed Colonel a little more, but then he stormed to free the stoneboat from the weeds and grass while the old man harnessed Colonel.

They hitched Colonel to the stoneboat, and Creek of her own accord came limping out of the barn and hobbled along with them toward the middle pasture where the welter of tornado junk rose queerly and desperately out of the rain-beaten grass. Creek looked odd in her long sock made out of folded-over, lapped-over feed sack. But she did not seem to mind the odd thing that covered even her hoof—not as long as she was with Colonel.

It was going to be a great day in the pasture

and in the sunshine. The pasture would get cleared and Grandpa's roof would go back on his house. And at the same time with the work and the liniment Colonel's legs would get limber and strong, and all the time Creek's cut in a sack that kept out the flies would be healing like mad—just like Dad in the hospital!

But this was still his birthday! Oh, what a day, and then the day to come with him and Mother talking and telling each other everything over two ice cream sodas, and maybe three. Mark had to blow his nose in his excitement, but that was from the strong liniment, because even in the open pasture Colonel reeked. Creek could hardly stand him, her nostrils flared, she coughed a little and hobbled away to graze in a clean stretch of grass.

Then came Mark's best birthday surprise from Grandpa. Instead of clearing a lane to Grandpa's roof, he loaded the stoneboat with beams and planks and with two-by-fours that he sorted out from the mess in the pasture. It turned out they were for Creek, for a stall for Creek right next to Colonel's. Last of all they piled slats on the stoneboat, because Creek was going to have a crib for hay and oats that would be a continuation of Colonel's crib, with no partition in between. "That's so they can nuzzle and feed together," Grandpa explained.

A stall for Creek! Mark could hardly believe it—that made it seem so sure that Creek was his and was going to stay. It seemed then that joy and hope could have no bounds, and one body could hardly contain it. Mark had to do all kinds of things at once, all things for Creek.

But Grandpa said, "Look, Grandson, stop going in five directions at one and the same time. I'll lay out the stall and measure things up, but you take Colonel and the stoneboat and get your dad's box of tools. We need tools to build that stall, and it'll be a good test for Colonel's legs before we use him to pull loads to clear the pasture. Take your time and don't hurry the old plug—it's going to be a long day. But if Colonel stumbles and falls, don't you mess around lifting his head to get him up on his feet again. Come back here and tell me."

Mark nodded obediently but scolded himself for having told Grandpa everything. It seemed that only he knew and believed that Colonel wouldn't ever hurt him. Colonel was careful for him.

He and Colonel trudged across the fields. It was an important day, and this an important errand—it was hard to go slow but Mark was careful for Colonel. To his relief, after the long, slow journey the tool box was still under the brush pile along Mason Road, exactly where he'd shoved it.

On the way back it was Colonel that hurried —he wanted to get back to Creek. And Mark wanted to get back to Grandpa and the building of Creek's stall. In spite of the fact that he'd thought he mustn't tell Grandpa everything, he thought of a thousand more things to tell on the long journey back from Mason Road.

When he and Colonel got back, Grandpa wasn't working on the stall, he was up in the hay loft, digging with the pitchfork at the hay-pile-play-pile with its tunnels. But Grandpa was careful of the tunnels, he only scraped hay from the rounded top of the pile. "It's for bedding for Creek. You can bring up a pitchfork and help me with this." When Mark came back up, the first thing he did was to dig right into the entrance of the small tunnel he had made the day of the tornado. Grandpa stopped him. "No, we can get plenty without wrecking your tunnels. I wouldn't mess them up for the world. A boy's got to have tunnels to get away from mothers and fathers fussing, and from horses with bad legs and wounds that won't heal fast enough, and dads in hospitals, and grandpas ordering him around."

Mark stopped his digging and looked at the old man in amazement and worship. How did he know the importance of tunnels?

"Did you have tunnels when you were a boy?" he asked hopefully.

"Nope, not being smart like you, I never thought of it. But I wish I had. And I wish last night I'd known you were under here. I'd have crawled in with you, and slept here too. Say!" Grandpa interrupted himself. "And just what is the matter with now—after the short sleep you and I had, and the long, scary, worrisome day, I could sleep right now, couldn't you? Creek's all right out there grazing with Colonel, and after a nap to take yesterday's tiredness out of our bones, we'll fix that stall for her better and faster than ever."

Grandpa threw his fork down and crawled into the wide old tunnel, the first one that Mark had ever made. Then Mark crawled into his small, yesterday's tunnel, stretched out full and sighed his pleasure and his delight—a grandpa in a tunnel. This was a birthday of birthdays. In the other tunnel Grandpa began to snore. Mark giggled but fell asleep in the middle of his giggle.

13

Grandpa Was Lonesome

It was the beginning of the second day of Grandpa and him alone on the farm. Mark wiped his mouth with the back of his hand. Now he'd eaten his second Grandpa-big breakfast, without napkins or orange juice. This time he'd had two cups of coffee. Mark drank it to the last bitter dregs. Awful as it tasted it was wonderful to drink the black brew, just like a man.

Now they were going out to fix Creek's leg and to sift oats for both horses. But when Mark stepped outside Grandpa wasn't behind him. Mark went back and found the old man going from room to room clicking on the light switches. But even though no light came Grandpa went to listen at the dead telephone and after that he switched on the radio and the television set—the blank screen seemed the deadest and blankest of all.

"What makes a man do silly, childish things like that? And me an old man!" Grandpa said scornfully. "You wouldn't have one here— you wouldn't have a battery radio? The batteries gave out on mine."

Mark shook his head.

They left the silent house that now seemed more dead than ever. "It's awful to know nothing of what's going on—just for the lack of a battery radio. I couldn't sleep for thinking about Mama. You know how it is when you can't sleep—it's got me down."

Mark looked away guiltily—he didn't know how it was, he had slept the whole night. He'd slept until Grandpa had shaken him awake for breakfast. He couldn't help it, after yesterday's big day of work.

"Come on, we've got to tend the horses." Grandpa acted as if he, Mark, had been holding them up.

He held the screen door for the old man, then he let it fall shut. It slammed, banged open and made a series of small flat slaps.

Grandpa stood on the steps listening, then said sharply, "Stop that blasted door. I can hear something. Listen! Sounds like the grinding of machinery."

Mark listened. "Yeah, it is. They must be clearing the highway."

"The highway? That's pretty far. Maybe they're through with the highway and are coming toward us."

Mark couldn't guess and neither could Grandpa. At last the old man moved away. "Come along, we'll tend to Creek and feed Colonel—by that time we'll know if the sounds are nearer and if they're coming toward us. Let's not get our hopes too high but if the highway is clear the buses will be running. We could walk to Stanton and get the bus from there into the city." Grandpa was so full of haste all of a sudden that Mark had to trot to keep up with him.

As they got to the barn Colonel neighed hungrily and tossed his hay around in his crib. Colonel didn't want hay. He wanted oats. He even stamped with his stiff old legs. "Look at that!" Grandpa said. "He's stamping. Guess the work and the liniment must be limbering him up—he's a work horse, he feels better with something to do."

Grandpa talked on about Colonel. It must

be so he, Mark, wouldn't notice Creek. She lay flat in her stall. She had kicked and worried the feed sack down around her hoof and though it was early morning the flies buzzed and hovered. It didn't make much difference for in no time she wore her hoof through the sack as she hobbled around.

"It's still so raw and infected I hate to pour anything in it," Grandpa muttered. "Think I'll wash it out with soapy water. She doesn't look as if she wanted to move around today so get me another sack and I'll tie it on after I get this washed out."

Mark darted to the corner shelf and came back with two. "This is all we've got left. She wears 'em out so fast and they're no good once she walks the whole bottom out."

"Two, hunh?" Grandpa said absently. "Well, we'll soon be getting to town and we'll pick up more. If we could find a veterinarian —but even then it'd probably be days before he could come out here. Well, I'll work on her, you run screen a pail of oats for Colonel."

"Two—one for Creek, too."

"If she'll eat. I doubt she will, but we can try. I think her mouth's too dry with fever. You run along—I'll give her some water if I

have to pour it down her from a kettle spout.
She's burning up."

"Is she going to die?" Mark blurted.

"Oh, no. A young horse doesn't die that
easy. I just wish we had a vet to shoot anti-
biotic in her. I don't like all the infection
but . . ." Grandpa suddenly glared up at him.
"Haven't you started out for oats yet?"

"Why are you so worried this morning?"
Mark stood his ground. "Has something bad
happened? If Creek isn't going to die, what is
it? Oh, Grandpa, is Dad going to die?"

Grandpa stood up. He was shocked. "Die!
Boy, what a question! What put that in your
head?"

Mark was startled himself. He said it but it
didn't mean anything. Dad was big and strong
and his father. You couldn't imagine your father could die.

At last Mark answered somberly. "I don't
know. But it's Colonel, isn't it? We worked
him too hard yesterday."

Grandpa shook his head but he didn't say
no. "Didn't you hear him neighing for oats?
And there you stand thinking up questions. If
the old horse dies it might be from hunger—
and you with that empty pail!"

Grandpa wanted to get rid of him. He started out with the empty pail.

After the long, slow sifting oats job Mark stopped in the kitchen to dig out one of his mother's trays. Grandpa had Creek all doctored up and bandaged—she smelled of the liniment. He must have poured some in her wound. Mark poured some of the oats in the flat tray and shoved it under Creek's head. Grandpa must have gone for water. Creek lay with her head in the tray but she made no effort to eat. Mark rubbed a handful of oats in her mouth but she sputtered them out again.

"I told you," Grandpa suddenly said behind him. "Her mouth and throat are too dry to choke down oats. I poured some water down her but with that fever I guess it's all burned up again. Her mouth is as dry as ever."

Mark stirred his fingers around in the oats but Creek jerked her head away.

Colonel whinnied jealously. He wanted the oats, he was hungry. It seemed hopeful that Colonel wanted to eat. Mark slid the oats out of the tray back into the pail and gave the whole pailful to Colonel, and the last of the vitamins, too. There were only three left. Colonel munched them with his worn old teeth. The way he was crunching oats made it seem a little unbelievable that he'd thought Colonel was going to die.

Grandpa had left the barn forgetting to give the pailful of water to Colonel—Mark couldn't lift it to the crib. He hurried out after Grandpa and found him in the house. Grandpa was going through the rooms clicking on switches.

"So you've caught me at it again." Grandpa looked a little guilty. "I hate to admit it but I'm so lonesome for Mama and so worried about her, I can't stand it any longer without news—it's as if we were on a desert island, not knowing what's going on. And I can't hear the machinery anymore. Could it be they've got our road cleared on the Stanton end?"

"I don't know," said Mark impatiently, "But Grandpa, I couldn't reach the pail of water up to Colonel, and shouldn't Creek have another drink?"

"Don't worry so. I'll give them both water but then you and I are going to start right out for Stanton. Who knows, maybe the buses are running again."

Mark couldn't say what he wanted, but he didn't want to leave Creek and Colonel. But if he had to go maybe he could find out whether Dad had bought Creek for him.

"Potatoes!" Mark suddenly yelled. "We'll feed Creek potatoes the way I fed them to Colonel. Cut potatoes are juicy and easy to swallow."

Grandpa sighed and got up. "Potatoes it is, then. We'll cut her some, but then it's straight to Stanton, or you're going to have to tie me up—at least put my feet in a feed sack and even then I think I'd hobble all the way to that hospital!"

They cut potatoes until Grandpa refused to do one more. "There's hardly any left anyway. If you're going to feed a horse potatoes, we ought to have a truckload."

"My dad's truck!" Mark was excited. "I'll bet it's still standing by the store he was building. We could go to town in Dad's truck and on the way back stop and get some potatoes."

"If it takes potatoes to get you away from your horses, then let's go look for that truck."

"It's for Creek," Mark pointed out. "If potatoes were good for Colonel, then they're good for Creek, too. Mother thought it up when I was so worried about Colonel, and it worked. It kept him alive when he was lying down so long and he liked them, they are slippery and nice."

Of course they didn't go until they fed almost the whole pailful to Creek, then Colonel got what was left over. "Maybe we should let them both out," Grandpa said.

"No," Mark said. "They've got to stay in the barn while we're gone." He was so worried about a man coming to claim Creek, taking her right out of the pasture, that he had no rest until Grandpa agreed to nail the barn door shut.

Grandpa hurried to the house and was already washed when Mark left the horses. That was all Grandpa could do, he couldn't change because all his other clothes were blown away in the tornado. He made Mark change into his Sunday clothes.

It turned out that the only part of the road to Stanton that was blocked was a long section starting at Grandpa's roofless house. The road lay full of uprooted trees, they had to go around them through the fields, then they walked down the gravel road to town.

Stanton was destroyed, the whole center of it where the stores were, even the brick bank was gone and the church where they'd found the man that was in the ambulance with Mama. Beyond that was the store his father had been building. The front half of the store lay in a tangle of wreckage. "Imagine, your father came out of that mess and is alive."

There among the wreckage, hardly banged up at all, stood Dad's truck. They had to pull away beams and window frames and planks and doors to get to it. Then Grandpa got up in the cab and started the motor. It roared and jolted forward, then Grandpa stopped it and Mark climbed up in the cab.

"Haven't driven a truck in twenty years," Grandpa yelled out above the roar. "It'll be a little jerky at first but hang on, driving is something you don't unlearn—even a truck."

With Grandpa wiggling the wheel the truck crawled slowly up the main street and then beyond the Stanton road there was a farmer's market already set up in the destruction. "There's potatoes," Mark screamed. "Stop!"

Grandpa searched for the brake. "Potatoes it is," he said. They bought all the potatoes the man would sell. "I've got to keep a few bushels for other people," he said. "You two can't hog all of them."

Grandpa didn't argue, he agreed and the potatoes were loaded on.

"I'm glad he didn't know they were for horses," Grandpa said as he started the truck.

Horses are important too, Mark thought but he didn't say it. He wiggled in the seat, glad of the potatoes. "I'm glad we didn't wait until we got back from the hospital, they might have been all gone."

Grandpa didn't answer. The truck just rolled straight on and at last Grandpa got used to it and dared to go fast down the highway.

As they were nearing the city Grandpa said, "Am I glad you thought of the truck. Not a single bus has passed us. Who knows where the tornado took them or in what kind of shape they are now?"

And Mark said, "We'll see Mother now in a minute and maybe Dad can tell us about Creek."

"Is there ever a moment you haven't your mind on horses?" Grandpa asked.

"Yes, it's sometimes on potatoes." Mark giggled. Then they both laughed and then they were driving into the parking lot of the hospital.

Mark had to run up the hospital steps to keep up with Grandpa.

He'd have to stay in the waiting room Grandpa said. "Kids can't go up where the sick folks are. A kid could give everybody the measles. Though in your case it'd be more likely to be bog spavins or hoof-and-mouth disease."

He rose out of sight in the elevator. Mark watched until it was gone, then dribbled to the waiting room. It was full of people. There wasn't one empty chair. A woman pointed out the windowsill and he had to sit there. His dangling legs wouldn't be still, they drummed the wall until a man in a chair reached out and stopped them. Then Mark sat motionless and waited and waited.

14

Ice Cream and Trucks

Mark tried to sit quietly, because the man next to him in the waiting room didn't seem to like his feet drumming the wall. It was difficult not to drum, he was so excited. Mark looked down at himself. Here he'd got dressed up in Sunday clothes because Grandpa had wanted it, but then they'd had to move planks and beams to free the truck, and then still load potatoes. Now in his Sunday suit and white shirt he was dirty as any ditch digger. But Mother hadn't seen him for so long, that, dirty as he was, he knew she would come in through the door of the waiting room and right away be mushy. Dirty as he was, she'd hug and hold him.

And there she was! She stood in the door-way, staring bewilderedly around at the full room. "Mother!" he yelled, and jumped from the windowsill and ran to her, but with his hand held out. They shook hands solemnly before all the waiting, staring people, then Mother just gathered him to herself and kissed and kissed him. Mark turned his face so he'd be looking toward the wall without watching people. But it was all right now, because the people had seen that it was Mother who had started it. He kissed her back.

"What a lucky time you picked to come," Mother exclaimed so loud that everybody must hear. "What a lucky time! Mark, just before I came down to you, your father spoke to me for the first time. He knew me right away!"

That was a silly thing to say before all the people. Why wouldn't Dad know Mother right off? She was his wife, she lived with him.

But Mother expected something from him, and so did the waiting people, at least the whole room had gone still. "He did? He did?" Mark squealed out. "What did he say? Mother, did he tell you about Creek, and whether he bought her, and Creek is mine?"

Mother looked puzzled—so she hadn't asked Dad. Mark almost wanted to push Mother backward through the door so she could run up again and ask about Creek. It was wonderful about Dad, but it was also important about Creek. Mother hadn't thought about somebody maybe claiming Creek.

Mother wouldn't shove, she still stood holding him tight. "Mother," he asked, muffled against her, "could you run up and quick ask?"

Mother looked at him in dismay. "Of course not! All they let him do was whisper to me. Know what that dad of yours said the first thing? 'Hello. I love you. How's Mark?'"

Mark stood guilty as she let him go, it was impossible to explain that he was terribly excited about Dad, but that at the same time Creek was his responsibility and worry. He stood dumb and miserable.

Mother understood. She kissed the top of his head, then said: "Here I was told by Grandpa you were going to take me out and buy me an ice cream soda."

"Come on, let's go," Mark yelped. "The first drugstore anywhere."

It turned out they could get their sodas right in the restaurant of the hospital. Before they went in, Mother first had to brush him. It didn't do much good, but it made her feel better. They sat at a little table across from each other and Mark ordered them each a double thick ice cream soda. He hoped Grandpa had given him enough money for double ice cream sodas.

He and Mother could hardly sip them at all for talking. There was so much to tell about Creek and Colonel, and the tornado and the milk wagon, and everything. Then Mark guessed he shouldn't have said so much about Creek's awful cut and the maggots. Mother listened, but she'd just quietly shoved her soda aside. It ended by Mark not having three sodas at all, just one and a half—his and what was left of Mother's.

Grandpa found them. Mark wanted to buy him a double chocolate soda, too, but Grandpa said, "No, make it coffee. I can stand anybody's after my own. But you have a soda along with me, and it looks as if your mother could stand coffee, too. What did you do to her to make her look so sort of green around the gills?"

"He's been talking maggots," Mother said from between thin lips. "But I thought you were going to stay up there while I was with Mark."

"They kicked me out," Grandpa said.

"They had to work on Mama. Just the same," he told Mark, "I got in a few quick words with your dad. He looks wonderful to me for a guy who had a roof caving down on his head. I knew you wouldn't have a minute's rest over Creek. I'm afraid, Mark, he didn't buy Creek."

Grandpa hastily turned to Mother. "That's another reason I came down," he told her. "The doctor said tomorrow both of them can come home—in an ambulance, of course. Mama will be in bed a long time. But he said with the day and night care you've been giving them, they'd actually be better at home, and this place is so overcrowded."

Their coffee came and Mother sipped gratefully at hers.

"So," Grandpa went on, "it looks like you ought to go home with Mark, and I will stay here. There's no roof on our house, and until there is, we'll have to stay with you, and there'll be lots to do to get ready for them. Can you drive a truck?"

"Me—a truck?" Mother almost rose out of her chair. "Well, I never have, and I hope I never have to."

"Don't say that so loud," Grandpa laughed, "because you're going to, if we're going to get those potatoes home for Creek and Colonel."

"Yes, Mom!" Mark said, letting go of the straw of his new soda. "It's just like with Colonel—Creek can only eat cut potatoes now, but she liked them just as much as old Colonel." It was sad but his tall glass of soda was just about empty, all but some thick dregs down in the bottom. He had to suck hard.

Grandpa jumped up. "I can't stand that slurping noise. Let's get out of here while he finishes that," he said to Mother. Mark looked up just in time to see him give Mother a significant nod. Grandpa knew he had seen it, because he immediately came back to the table and said, "Say, Mark, when they kicked me out of Mama's room, I went to your dad's. It's all right about the maggots—they keep a wound clean. He said he'd learned that in the war. So no sacks or anything, but keep it out in the air and sunshine and all the flies that want to come."

There were no words to say to that amazing thing.

Grandpa abruptly walked to Mother. Mark still had to pay for the coffee and sodas. He went to the cashier, but though he stood quite near them, Mark could only hear a word now and then of what Grandpa was saying to Mother. But that word seemed to be "Colonel" —again and again. Did it mean Colonel was going to die? The chocolate sodas rose up in his throat and Mark shoved his money at the cashier and turned away without waiting for his change.

Mother and Grandpa turned to him. "It's all arranged," Mother said hastily. "Grandpa and I talked it over, and he's right, I should be there on the farm getting things ready. Grandpa is going to drive the truck to the outskirts of town, and then I'll take over. Grandpa wants to walk back and buy a clean shirt and trousers, otherwise he's afraid they won't let him stay—it's such a clean hospital."

"But I thought you couldn't drive a truck." Mark searched their faces.

Grandpa turned away. "I'll go get the truck and meet you at the foot of the steps."

"It looks like I'll have to drive the truck," Mother told Mark as they walked out of the hospital. "You see, I haven't got our car here. It's wherever I left it in Stanton. I got to Stanton just after the tornado had struck, and I abandoned the car to run to the store where Dad was working. I got there as they were putting him into an ambulance, and I sat on the floor with his poor head in my lap all the way to the hospital."

Grandpa roared up with the truck, and it was no use then to ask the dreaded question about Colonel.

Mother sat between Mark and Grandpa in the high cab of the truck and watched everything Grandpa did. Mark sat still and worried.

At last they were near the outskirts of town, and on a quiet street, before getting to the highway, Grandpa got down and made Mother drive while he sat next to her and watched her. "You see, it's no different from a car," he told her. "Only your moves and twists and turns can't be quite as abrupt. But don't worry, you're in a truck, and if anything gets in your way, just lean on your horn. If anybody says anything, just look down from your cab and give him some truck driver talk out of the side of your mouth."

Mother laughed nervously. Then Mark had to open the door and let Grandpa down over him. Grandpa kneaded his shoulder as he stepped down. "Now, Grandson, don't worry so, just remember that no horse has ever been loved like that before. That he's had, and that you've had, so be grateful."

Mark nodded dumbly—words like that always wanted to make the tears come. Then Grandpa slammed the door shut and was gone. The truck roared into motion.

It was miles before Mother stopped wiggle-waggling the big steering wheel. At last she leaned back and sat in the seat, instead of wrestling the steering wheel, perched on the edge of the seat like a canary on a stick.

She laughed a little and brushed her hair back. "It's just like Grandpa said, it's not too much different from a car. Another mile and I'll be talking out of the side of my mouth."

"Another two miles and we'll be home," Mark said somberly. "Mother, Grandpa told you Colonel was going to die, didn't he?"

Mother made believe something was in her way down the road, she leaned toward the windshield. "It's nothing, just a dog, I guess," she muttered. Then, looking straight ahead, she said, "Grandpa doesn't know for sure. He only thinks so, he only guesses. Grandpa isn't God, anymore than you or I. Your father and the old farmer thought that Colonel would have died long ago, and still he's here, and through a tornado. And look at all the potatoes we are bringing him."

Mother's words were just words, but he

mustn't worry her now going down the Stanton Road, so narrow with piled ridges of stuff from the tornado. "Hey, linemen!" Mark exclaimed. "They're putting up the lines again."

Mother was sitting like a bird on a perch again, worrying and waggling the wheel down the narrow road. Mark told her: "Colonel ate the biggest meal of oats in his life this morning."

They were just words too. Even he did not believe his brave-sounding voice, and neither did Mother. But they had to leave the road and go between Grandpa's roofless house and the gone barn, and it needed all Mother's attention. Now there was only the single field to get home to Colonel.

"Home!" Mother said. "And it's still there, and we're still here—even Colonel. Oh, Mark, can't we be more thankful?"

Mark nodded his head, but it was false—he couldn't be thankful.

15

The Colonel Tree

They parked the truck behind the house, and Mother leaped from the high cab even before Mark could get down, and she ran to the house as if she had not been there for weeks. But in the kitchen she stopped in her tracks and just looked: "No wonder Grandpa wanted me home! What a mess, what an unholy mess! Two days, and this! Here I've got to get everything for your dad and Mama—and I'm faced with a week's work in this kitchen. I declare, before I do a thing I'm going to build a pigsty outdoors for you and Grandpa."

Mark threw her a sheepish grin but he'd no time for all that. He grabbed the claw hammer from among the dishes next to the sink. "Help me get the barn door open," he said. "I can't reach the high nails—hurry."

Mother came. Mark ripped out the lower nails, but Mother had a struggle with the high ones and Mark stood impatiently. It was taking too long, and Colonel wasn't neighing a welcome as he always did when he first heard Mark.

"Whatever did you and Grandpa nail up the door for?" Mother demanded in her struggles.

"So nobody could come and take Creek away," Mark answered shortly.

"But Mark, you must face it. Sooner or later someone is almost bound to claim Creek —unless her owners were killed."

"It isn't Creek now, it's Colonel." As he said that the last nail came away and he slid the door open.

Colonel wasn't dead, but he didn't neigh out or turn to Mark. He just rested on his threshing-machine straps. He pawed one foot impatiently. "He wants to get out, he wants to get out of the barn," Mark told Mother.

Creek had got up but she'd eaten no potatoes. Mark dashed in beside her and slid Mother's tray out of sight under the hay. He pulled up Creek's feed sack. Dad said it wasn't needed, but Mother had better not see. Mother was beside Colonel. "Why don't we put Creek in Colonel's stall since he wants to go outside?

She could rest her leg if you put the straps under her. I don't think Colonel will want Creek hobbling after him now."

Mark rushed into Colonel's stall and helped let down the straps. Yes, Creek would be easier if she could rest without putting weight on her cut leg.

But Colonel couldn't wait. By himself he stumbled out of the barn and went through the gateway into the pasture.

They stood looking after him. "I guess he wants to be alone, or maybe just with you," Mother's voice was shaky.

Grandpa had seen it this morning, now Mother must have seen it too. Colonel was going to die.

Mother would not let him ask the question. "Mark," she said. "I know what I'll do, I'll cut up potatoes for Creek. I can't *stand* being in that house the way . . . Look, Colonel's looking back for you. If you need me I'll be right here on the truck—just yell out and I'll come."

Mark ran to Colonel. Colonel turned his head and looked out of the corner of his eyes but he didn't wait. He started down the length of the pasture.

Mark ran back to the truck. "I'm going to

stay with Colonel. I think he wants to go to his creek. I'll go with him because he's going to die. He told me just now when he looked at me."

Mother cleared her throat and put one hand on Mark's shoulder. "Yes, I thought he told me too, there in the stable. But animals don't always know—neither do we. It could be he just needs to walk or to stand in the creek, he's heading that way. I've got some potatoes cut up, why don't you take them with you for Colonel?"

Mark started off with the pan, a little stumbly.

"Mark, I don't know," Mother called, "do you want me along or would you rather be alone?"

Mark turned. He wanted to thank her but his voice wouldn't come. Finally he croaked out, "Alone."

"Mark! Colonel's down. He fell just now," she jumped from the truck, almost fell herself and came running. She grabbed Mark's hand. He dropped the pan of potatoes and together they ran.

Mother and Mark stroked the long white cheek of Colonel as he lay with his head flat to the ground. But Colonel looked only at Mark.

"You stay with him," Mother said. "I'll run back and get the potatoes and you can feed them to him one by one."

Mark shook his head. "No, Mother, we don't need the potatoes."

Mother sighed. "I guess you don't need me either." She stroked Colonel once more and walked away.

Now Mark and Colonel were alone—a long time they were alone. Mark could see Mother watching from the truck. He told Colonel many important things and then he said them all over again. Colonel listened and slid his head back and forth in the grass until there was no more to say, no more need to listen. Then he warned Mark with his eyes. He did it so suddenly, so unexpectedly, that Mark had to jump back and out of the way. Colonel threw himself up, first his head and then his forelegs, and then in one great heave all of him came up. Colonel was on his feet! He staggered away a few steps and looked around to see if Mark was coming. Mark grabbed the end of the halter rope and immediately Colonel set off down the pasture. He was heading for the creek in the woodlot, Colonel wanted to stand in his cool creek.

It was too far. Mark told Colonel over and

over that it was too far, but Colonel kept going. They would never get there, never reach the creek. Colonel was stumbling.

Mark tugged desperately at the rope and slowly Colonel turned with him toward the spring in the bank of catalpas. "The spring doesn't run and whisper," Mark told Colonel softly, "but it's cool there in the grass and you can drink."

Colonel listened and they went to the nearby spring that on this sunny afternoon was deep-shadowed by the catalpas growing on the bank. They walked very slowly for with the spring so close there seemed all the time in the world. All the time in the world in the sadness that lay over the sunshiny land.

They got to the spring. There Colonel lay down in the cool wet grass shaded by the catalpas. He wanted a drink. He couldn't lift his head but his eyes went to the drops of water dripping from the end of the pipe. Mark measured the distance with his eyes. Colonel's head was near the spring. There was a length of old tubing in the barn—if he could slip it over the pipe, he could lead water into Colonel's mouth.

He raced to the barn, waving to Mother that everything was all right.

The tubing was long enough. It slid over the end of the pipe and was soft enough to squeeze between Colonel's lips. Colonel drank. He swallowed the trickle-drip that collected around his teeth and flowed into his mouth. Then Colonel swallowed once more, spit out the tube, looked up at Mark—and died.

Mark dropped the tubing, kneeled down and kissed Colonel. He sat in the wet grass beside his horse. There was no one but the two of them. Mother couldn't see him crying. Even if she could, he wouldn't call or wave. He had to sit here a little while.

At last he got up and walked away but he didn't go to the truck. He went to the barn to get two shovels. When he came back Mother was standing beside the truck, searching the pasture with her eyes. He raised the shovels as a sign to her. Mother came.

Mark waited ramrod straight, as if his two shovels were shouldered rifles. He told her, "Colonel died. We have to bury him."

"Yes," Mother said. "We knew, didn't we?"

Mark marched beside her like a grave old man. "You and I. We'll bury him because we both loved him."

They talked no more. They walked around Colonel and Mother studied how he lay. "It'll be easy here under the spring. The ground is soft and I think it's sandy." Her voice was calm and low and steady. "It was wonderful of Colonel to pick this spot."

"He wanted to go to his creek but I turned him away, and he came."

Mother dug the first shovelful of sod. Mark went behind Colonel and began digging too, he could not quite face Colonel yet. When he looked up Mother had hunched down and closed Colonel's eyes, and she closed his lips over his big teeth.

Then she came around to Mark with her shovel. "You're doing it right—I'm wrong. If we both dig behind him, all the way along his back, then with Colonel's weight on the edge of . . ." she hesitated, then she said it, "with his weight on the edge of the grave, I think there'll be a cave-in and Colonel will slide down with the sand."

The hardest digging was the sod. Mother dug and Mark piled it as she dug. "No, don't pile the sod against the bank," she cautioned. "Pile it above Colonel's head, because as we dig deep, unless the catalpa roots hold it, the whole bottom of the bank may come down to slide over Colonel. And we want the sod to cover the grave, don't we?"

Mark nodded. "Then last of all we'll plant a cross," he told her softly. "There's all those beams in the pasture—I'll make a cross."

Mother looked up in surprise but she said nothing.

After the sod, the moist sand threw out easily but the moisture made the sand stick together so it stayed in place and there was no early cave-in. The threat of a cave-in grew as the hole deepened and went into the bank. They both kept a wary eye on the straight side of the grave along Colonel's back—all of Colonel's weight was bearing down on it.

Now the enormous hole was almost deep enough. Mark started digging up into the bank but Mother kept turning toward Colonel.

The cave-in came with silent swiftness the way a snake or a weasel comes. There was no time to call out a warning, only time to catch Mother's hand and help pull her up on the bank where he'd been digging. Even then Mother had to wrench one leg out of the silent-flowing sand as Mark tugged her up. Then they were safely on the grass and Mother turned Mark away and pressed his face against her. Mark jerked away to look. Colonel settled on his side down in the hole among the flowing sand. Mark began to cry.

"Now we'll need that cross. Can you make it now?"

Mark nodded, fisted away his tears and started to run.

"I'll stay here and rest awhile," Mother said. "It was such hard work."

But when Mark turned to look back, Mother was not resting, she was digging into the bank. She wanted the sandy bank to slide down over Colonel.

Mark watched her uncertainly, not knowing whether to run back and help or to go on. That moment the whole bank came streaming, rolling down. It covered Colonel. A small catalpa, low on the bank, slid down in the flowing sand until it stopped upright in the middle of Colonel's grave.

"Mark! Mark!" Mother called. "Come look! A little tree came down to Colonel."

Mark came racing. "The little tree planted itself over Colonel," Mother said excitedly. "A little live tree—we don't need a cross now, do we?"

"Oh, no," Mark said. "A cross won't grow, but the little tree will."

"Then it's going to be the Colonel Tree," Mother said. "It's going to grow and be the Colonel Tree."

Mark nodded. Then suddenly he had to sit down on one of the sods. He was so drained, so spent. He couldn't even help Mother lay the sod. At last Mother finished. She had not needed the sod he was sitting on. Cautiously she straightened her back, and Mark could hear the weariness creak up out of her stoop.

He did not get up. "Colonel died," he said, "and Dad didn't get Creek for me. Now if they come to claim Creek, I won't have anything." He sat a moment. Suddenly he bawled out at her. "How can I wait and wait—days and days —until they come and get Creek?"

Mother stood spent. At last she said, "I'm too tired to think now. But there must be something we can do. Let's go home, let's rest for a while. Maybe I can think of something."

Mark nodded wearily, and took her hand.

They walked away together—they let the shovels lie.

16

"A Horse Came Running"

Mother and Mark walked the whole way home in silence and sadness. Mark had no words, and Mother just plunged straight ahead, she seemed to be thinking deep. But when they reached the house yard, suddenly she started running—the telephone inside the house was ringing.

"The phone!" Mark yelled. "The lines are up. They finished putting up the lines on the Stanton Road."

Mother ran through the kitchen and its mess without seeing anything but the telephone. She grabbed the receiver, but when she answered, it was only a lineman testing. She hung up and stood there. Suddenly she grabbed the telephone directory and fluttered the pages. "But now I know what to do—now that we have a telephone," she exclaimed. "I'll call the radio station."

She found her number and dialed the phone. Over the phone Mother explained to a loud-speaking man the thing that had happened with Creek running to the farm the night of the tornado, and now the death of Colonel.

"So couldn't I make a radio appeal?" she begged. "Couldn't I make it right over the telephone, and you broadcast it all over, so that if the horse that came running to us is to be claimed, it would be claimed now—instead of our waiting and waiting and never knowing?"

Hanging on to the silent receiver, Mother turned to Mark and hurriedly explained. "It came to me the moment I heard our phone ringing!" She snapped her fingers. "Just like that, I thought I could make an appeal on the radio, the way I did from town the night of the tornado, with your dad unconscious in the hospital, and me not knowing what had happened or what would become of you."

The phone made abrupt loud noises, Mother listened again. At last she turned back to Mark. "The announcer is going to say word for word over the radio exactly what I say to him on the phone, and everywhere people will hear. Maybe Creek's owner too—if he's still alive—and then he will come, and maybe we can persuade him to sell Creek to us."

Amazement and hope made Mark speechless.

"They're setting things up, and the moment the present broadcast is over, they're going to let me make my appeal," Mother explained so Mark would understand the wait.

At last the telephone crackled and sputtered, and Mother held the receiver so tight to her ear, her ear went dead white. "They're ready for me," she said in a panicky voice. "What will I say—how will I say it?"

Over the telephone the announcer's voice laughed, and Mother had to start talking. Mark couldn't stand there any longer, he raced away to the living room. There—the way Grandpa had done—he clicked on the radio. But now it worked, the electricity was back again, the electric lines were up too. Mark couldn't yell it to Mother—she was talking. In a slow voice, because his words were going everywhere, the announcer began to repeat Mother's words. Standing between the radio and the kitchen Mark could hear them both.

"A horse came running to our farm the night of the tornado," Mother said into the phone. "A horse came running," the announcer began.

"A horse came running," Mother repeated, then she stopped confused. "Oh, I already said that." Mother began again. "Its leg had been terribly cut in the tornado, and now it is crippled. My boy found her, and he named her Creek. Colonel is—was—the name of my son's own horse. Was, because Colonel died, and we just now buried him. Now all there is left is Creek, but we don't own her. We want to own her now that Colonel is gone. Even crippled, we'd buy her." Mother hesitated. Then firmly she said. "Yes, we will buy her for a fair price because my boy needs her now."

The announcer broke in. "Lady, describe the horse so the owner will recognize her."

"Oh, how shall I do that?" Mother's voice went wobbly. "She's thin and raggedy now, and run down from her wound, but she was a sleek all-over brown, except for a white blaze, a sort of star running down her forehead. A star—well, like the Star of Bethlehem is always pictured, you know, with sort of long rays going down. Creek's star sort of rays down that way toward her nose."

"That's good enough," the announcer interrupted. "Don't try any more, because that is perfect. Now just your address, and anybody that ever owned a horse with a Bethlehem Star will know. And all over the countryside, I can tell you, we will hope and wait with you and your boy. Be sure to let us know what develops."

Mark ran to Mother. In a choked, spent voice Mother was giving their address, then slowly she hung up the receiver as if it were leaden and heavy. Together they went to the living room and Mark shut off the radio. It had to be still now in the house, it had to be still so as to take it all in and run it over in his mind. Mother sat on the couch beside him, and she too needed to rest and be still. She took Mark's hand in hers.

They waited and waited until waiting became impossible in the stillness of the telephone, and in the sadness over Colonel, and the tenseness over Creek. Lumped in a hard ball inside of all that stood the hard fear of losing Creek.

Mark stirred, wrung his hand out of Mother's nervous hold, and jumped up. "I can't be still like this, I've got to do something—I'm going to exercise Creek. I'll just go with her up and down the lane because from there I can see if anybody comes, and I can hear if you call me when somebody telephones."

"Yes, do," Mother said. "And I'll straighten the house while waiting for the telephone, if I'm not to sit here screaming. Telephone ring! Anything, anybody, just so we know it still works. The lines may still be up so poorly that nobody can call us now—maybe anything, you can think anything, if you keep sitting still." Mother jumped up. "Let's get to work."

Mark ran from the house. In the barn, before letting down the straps from under Creek, he pulled the feed sack off her leg. Dad knew, and now the sock shouldn't be on—maggots were good!

As he worked on Creek, Mark kicked against the tray he had hid from Mother under the bedding hay. Creek did not want to back out of the stall, she did not seem to want to move. Mark let her stand and flew to the truck and its cut potatoes with Mother's tray.

As Mark had hoped, the potatoes tempted Creek. He gave her none, but held the tray out before him, chest high, and once Creek was turned around, she hobbled after him, head over his shoulder trying to reach the potatoes on the tray. That way they walked the length of the lane, Creek munching potatoes out of the tray.

When they returned and came past the barn, there down the road came a car drawing a horse trailer behind it. It stopped at their driveway. Two men got out of the car. Mark stood there, he couldn't move, he stood frozen with apprehension. Then Mother came out of the house and he went to her with Creek. Creek tried to reach the last potato on the tray.

Mark and Creek got to the house at the same time as the two men. It *was* Creek's owner—Creek's owner with a veterinarian he had brought along with him. He explained it to Mother. "I tried to call, but your telephone isn't right." Abruptly the man turned to Creek. He looked and looked as if he couldn't believe his eyes. "In just three days, that's all that's left of her?" he asked hoarsely. "Can a wound run a horse down that fast?" he demanded of the veterinarian.

"If it's bad enough and infected enough, like this one looks to be, yes," the veterinarian said.

"But all that's left of her is ribs and hide and

a hollow back and a maggoty wound!" The owner crouched down to study the deep cut. Abrputly he rose, turned away from Creek, and stayed turned away.

Mark stared at him, unbelieving. He did not want to look at Creek at all. He didn't love her. He was only angry because she had a cut leg. He was not a good man.

The owner turned to the veterinarian. "You look at her."

It didn't take the veterinarian long, then he too straightened up. "The tendon's cut, that's sure," he said. "So unless you want to keep her as a pet, she'll never be good again for riding."

"Pet!" The man spat, his face twisting. "Do you realize I had that horse at my place only a good two days? I'd just bought her. And what I paid for her! And now keep her as a crippled pet?" He spat again.

"I hate to tell you this," Mother said, "but they told us the maggots are good. We tried to keep them out with bandages, but they said the wound would heal better in the open air."

The veterinarian looked his surprise, but told the man, "She's right. When there's nothing else at hand maggots are good. Don't let them bother you. They're keeping the wound clean, keeping it healing. But, of course, they can't bring back a cut tendon."

The man didn't listen. He walked down the drive without looking back. "Bring the horse," he called over his shoulder, "and load her on the trailer. Then shoot her. I don't want to see her again. I'll get my girl another horse. Three days—and that!"

The veterinarian shrugged and looked at Mother. "I'm afraid a tornado doesn't first look at the cost of what it's going to wreck."

Mark stood horrified, looking after the man walking to his car. Did he really have a gun in the car? Were they going to shoot Creek right here and now? "Mother!" he croaked.

In big steps Mother went down the driveway, then stopped and called out, "You stop right there. We'll buy Creek as she is, for what in decency you care to ask. She came here, she stays here, if you're going to shoot her, she's not yours anymore. She's my boy's—he loves her."

Mark snatched Creek's halter rope away from the veterinarian. "She's mine," he yelled. "She's mine—she came to me."

The man at the car turned and looked at him. "Okay, son, she's yours, but not for money. I wouldn't sell anything I don't want myself. Consider her a gift from me to some-body that wants her like that. Keep your Creek —she's yours."

The veterinarian came up beside Mark, pummeled him with a soft fist. "Good," he said. "Just keep exercising her. And I'll be back to work on your Creek as soon as I can get rid of *him*."

Mark could not say a word. It couldn't be believed, it couldn't be endured—not standing still. "Mother," he whispered, "he said Creek was mine. She's mine, and it's forever."

Then he had to run, but he ran to the truck and pulled down more potatoes for Creek's tray. He started up the lane. Creek came hob-bling after him, head reaching over his shoul-der to get at the tray. Then Mother came.

They walked and walked up the lane, down the lane, for walking was the only thing to do in happiness like this. Walking was the only way to wait. Next the veterinarian would come and work on Creek. But the veterinarian knew, as Mother did, that he did not need a perfect horse—he needed Creek.

Then they'd wait still some more, but then Grandpa would come, bringing Dad and Mama in the ambulance. The great news about Creek would be waiting for them. The moment that they came he'd be in the driveway to yell out the news, so that Dad, Grandpa and Mama would know even before they opened the ambulance door.

Thinking like that, even walking was not enough for Mark. He had to run. Mother understood. She took the tray of potatoes from him and walked on with Creek down the lane. Mark ran across the pasture and down to the gully of the fallen tree with the big crotch. He touched the crotch as he passed it in his running, then ran hard from the gully into the woodlot and into Colonel's creek. He splashed hard all the way down the creek until he emerged at the lane end of the woodlot. He'd run so fast that Mother was only now coming to the end of the lane with Creek. He hugged her and kissed her, and then he kissed Creek. He took the tray from Mother, and Creek walked with her munching head down over his shoulder again. Wait till they heard, wait till they heard!

"Creek's mine," he had to say to Mother in his wonder. Mother put her arm around his shoulder. And so they walked, and walked, and walked.